Acknowledgments and Thanks

I wish to thank the following people for their support and devotion as I wrote this novel.

- My God
- My Family
- My Country

Jackpine Strong

Skip Coryell

Published by White Feather Press. (www.whitefeatherpress.com)

ISBN 978-1-61808-178-0

Printed in the United States of America

Cover photo man with gun ©iStockphoto.com/ PaSta77
Back cover photo of pine trees, courtesy of Rick Vuyst
Front cover photo of pine trees, courtesy of Rick Vuyst

White Feather Press

Reaffirming Faith in God, Family, and Country!

Books by Skip Coryell

We Hold These Truths
Bond of Unseen Blood
Church and State
Blood in the Streets
Laughter and Tears
RKBA: Defending the Right to Keep and Bear Arms
Stalking Natalie
The God Virus
The Shadow Militia
The Saracen Tide
The Blind Man's Rage
Civilian Combat - The Concealed Carry Book
Jackpine Strong

For Sara, my dear wife,
whom I love and fight for.

And to my children.

From the author

When I first started writing *Jackpine Strong*, it was going to be my very first romance novel. That fantasy lasted for about 60 pages. My wife, Sara, who was reading it had to break the bad news to me. "Honey, I'm sorry, but this is not a romance novel." When I asked why, she said, "You keep killing off all the characters." She was kind enough to explain to me that most women don't find murder, death and mayhem to be very romantic. *Oddly enough, that thought had never occurred to me.*

So, my romance novel suddenly morphed into a crime drama, but I'm okay with that. It freed me up to be myself and stop talking about tender feelings all the time. So ladies, unless you have a tolerance for murder, death and mayhem, you may not appreciate it this novel as much as I do. But guys ... you're going to love it!

Regardless of your affinity for violence, I hope you enjoy my story. The good characters are packed with virtue, courage and morality. The bad characters are downright evil, and, in the end, they get what they deserve. And you certainly can't ask for more than that!

So, it is with great pleasure that I bring to you the first book in the Jack Ruger Adventure Series. And for those of you who don't know "Jack," better hang on tight, because it's a real wild ride!

Skip Coryell

CHAPTER 1

Jackpine - Extreme Northern Michigan

SARA SINAI WAS A HANDSOME BRUnette. Her features were pronounced, as if chiseled in a stonelike visage from the gods themselves. Everyone thought Sara was attractive.

She typed away on the computer, but then reached down to move the mouse for just a second. Her hands were large and strong, speckled in dark hair, jutting up from her skin like an uncontrolled briar patch, even out to the furthest knuckle of her fingers. Sara Sinai was thirty-six years old. She was six feet three inches tall and weighed in at one-hundred and eighty-five pounds. But her attractiveness ran much deeper than the hairy skin that covered almost her entire body. Sara also had a kind heart and a warm smile.

She suddenly felt chilled, so she pulled the pink bath robe in closer and wrapped it tightly around her. She moved the soft, fuzzy collar up to her nose and smelled it; she could smell nothing, and the absence brought her grief. But what could she expect? It had been over a year now. Sara read the text out loud to get a feel for how it would play with her readers.

> Abigail moved in closer and snuggled in even tighter to Remington's gentle embrace. As

they held one another on the park bench, Abigail watched her young daughter play happily on the swings with the other children. She looked up and saw Remington watching as well. He looked down at her and smiled

"I love you, Abby. I love your daughter, and I can't wait for us to be a family together."

And then he got down on one knee, and held her slender hand in his own as he looked up into her face longingly.

"Please Abby ... Please be my wife and make all my dreams come true."

Tears streamed down Abigail's face, as she opened her mouth to speak, but ... nothing came out. So she simply nodded her head up and down at first. Then, her happiness finally found voice.

"Yes, yes, yes, a thousand times yes, Remington! What took you so long?"

Abigail pulled him up from his knees and he picked her up off the ground and kissed her passionately. Abigail's body reacted as her face grew flushed and hot.

All around her, the children were playing and the robins were singing, but she didn't hear them. They were simply the background music for her own ... happily ever after.

Finally ... she had found someone to love.

Sara finished reading from the computer screen and smiled, then she reached up and ran her fingers through her coarse, brunette hair. She pressed "control s" to save, and then smiled one more time before closing the laptop. It was perfect, and she would finish the formatting and get it up for sale on Amazon later. But ... for now, she'd have just enough time to get to work.

Sara walked down the hall and into the bathroom, where she let the pink robe fall unfettered to the floor. She turned on the hot water, let it warm up a few seconds and then stepped in to let the warm water hit her body. It was like this every time she wrote; it was almost as if she were a different person.

CHAPTER 2

AMANDA **W**ALKER LOVED THE world of publishing. She loved the fast pace of New York City, along with all the night life and the friends, and the parties, the interesting people and even the busy traffic, the noise and the smell of car exhaust. Yes, Amanda had been tailor-made for big-city life, and there was no place she'd rather be than right here at her desk, brokering million-dollar book deals and meeting with the famous authors of the future. She was making history, and she loved it.

There was a soft knock on her door before it opened, followed closely by her assistant, Roxanne.

"Amanda, sorry to interrupt, but ... Mr. Harvath wants to see you in his office right away. He said whatever you're doing right now can wait."

Amanda looked up from her laptop, puzzled. "Really? Is something wrong?"

Roxanne just shrugged her shoulders. "I don't know, boss, but he looked pretty tense to me."

Amanda's eyebrows raised in surprise. "He came down here just to tell you to tell me to go to his office? Why didn't he just call?"

"I don't know, but I saw him at the copy machine. He flagged me down and wasn't very nice about it. I don't think he's mad, but ..." She threw up her hands and turned to leave. "If I was you I wouldn't wait too long." The door closed behind her.

Amanda scrunched her brow and thought for a moment. For the life of her she couldn't recall anything she'd done wrong. Why would he be so upset at her? Finally, she decided the only way to find out was to go see him.

Bedrock publishing was one of the largest in the United States. It wasn't the biggest, but it certainly was one of the top five players in the publishing world. Amanda walked out of her office and past her assistant, who seemed to be avoiding her stare. She glanced over at the coffee makers in the break room and saw Tina, one of her staunchest competitors. Tina and Amanda had a lot in common. They were both in their late twenties, both drop-dead gorgeous, and both incredibly ambitious. She tried to slip on by without Tina noticing, but luck was not on her side today.

"Hey Amanda, how's it going girl?"

But Amanda didn't slow down. She simply waved her left hand as she walked by. "Can't talk right now, Tina. Got an important meeting with Mr, Harvath. Something really big."

Tina kept moving toward her, but Amanda was too fast. As she approached the elevator, it was already beginning to close, but Amanda rushed forward as quickly as her high heels would carry her and made it in time before it closed behind her.

Alone inside for a few seconds, she looked in the mirror on the wall beside her and checked her make-up. Her long, honey-blonde hair spiraled down in soft waves. Most women had to make their hair look this way by spending hours at the beauty parlor, but Amanda just had to wake up and run a brush through it. She'd been kissed with a natural beauty, and she looked impeccable, as always.

When the elevator door opened, she walked directly up to Ms. Robinson's desk, just outside her bosses' office. The older woman, with greying hair and spectacles on her nose didn't even look up at her. That always bothered Amanda, but there was nothing she could do about it.

"Mr. Harvath is waiting for you, Miss Walker. You may go right in."

Amanda nodded. "Thank you Ms. Robinson." The older woman didn't look up as Amanda knocked softly and then continued on into her bosses' office. That was the way he liked it, and had told her so on several occasions when she'd tried to do it differently.

Mr. Harvath was with a man from contracts. They were both hunched over some papers, talking in hushed legalese. They appeared not to notice her, but Amanda knew better. She maintained her distance, waiting until they formally recognized her. After two or three minutes the man from contracts got up and left the office. He ignored Amanda on his way out.

"Amanda. Thanks for coming. Please sit."

The tone of her boss was hurried and stressed. He was about fifty pounds overweight, balding head, and only five feet six inches tall. Despite all that, he carried himself with dignity and command. His grey, pinstripe suit was tailor-made for his egg-shaped frame, and was the perfect wrapping for him.

"You called for me, sir."

Amanda was seated now in front of his desk. Mr. Harvath took one final look at the paper contract in front of him, then put it back inside a clear plastic folder. He got right to the point.

"I have a very important job for you, Amanda. I need you to go somewhere and sign a new author."

Amanda crossed her legs, being careful not to show too much of her upper thigh, because she knew that Mr. Harvath didn't appreciate that kind of thing.

"Sure. I can do that for you, sir. Where am I going?"

Mr. Harvath didn't speak. Instead, he slid the folder across his desk to her. She picked it up, a questioning gaze on her face. He simply nodded to her, and she took that to mean she was to open the folder and read.

"Michigan, sir?"

Mr. Harvath nodded.

"Who is Sara Sinai? I've never heard of her."

Mr. Harvath smiled and leaned back in his big, soft and comfortable office chair.

"She's a romance writer who just hit number one on Amazon. In fact, this is her third number one romance this year alone."

Amanda looked up from the contract. "Really. Who did she publish with?"

Mr. Harvath shook his head from side to side. "No one. She self-published through Amazon."

Amanda looked back down at the contract. She quickly scanned through it and was surprised to see the six-figure offer. They must really want this woman. Right now it was Tuesday, only two days before Thanksgiving. But she had no plans other than rest, relaxation and partying with her friends.

"If you're too busy, Amanda, I can give this job to Tina. I know this is a holiday." He hesitated and watched her reaction. "Do you have family plans already?"

She quickly closed the folder, uncrossed her legs and laid it on her lap. "No sir. I'd be happy to do this. When do I leave?"

Mr. Harvath leaned forward in his chair and reached over to the left side of his desk. His desk was always neatly organized, with piles that were assembled and stacked in a priority that only he could decipher. He picked up a legal-sized envelope and tossed it over to her.

"Your travel itinerary, tickets, destination and everything we know about Sara Sinai is in this envelope."

Amanda picked it up and placed it on her lap with the contract. Her boss then reached into the right, top drawer of his mahogany desk and pulled out three paperback books.

"These are her best-sellers. I want you to read them during the flight. Get to know her. Her writing isn't like anything else we've seen. In fact, we're thinking it may be a whole new sub-genre to the romantic fiction market. And it's got legs, Miss Walker. This woman is an unknown. She skyrocketed to the top of the list without any money being spent, with zero marketing. Her rise is truly organic."

Amanda picked up the books and looked at the covers. The cover stock was thin, the binding was cheap, and the cover design was unprofessionally done.

"These are number one on Amazon?"

Mr. Harvath nodded slowly. Just read them, Miss Walker. Then, if you're as smart as I think you are ... then you'll understand what we're dealing with here."

Amanda looked up and smiled softly. "Why, thank you, sir." She waited a moment before getting up. "Will that be all, Mr. Harvath?"

Her boss didn't say anything. He just looked at her, then he turned to gaze out his big, corner window at the Manhattan skyline. "Do you like working here at Bedrock, Miss Walker?"

Amanda tried not to squirm in her chair, but failed slightly. "Yes, sir. I like it very much."

The man across from her nodded slowly. "Good. Our competitors will try to sign her as well. But that can't happen. This client will make or break your career in the publishing industry, Miss Walker." He paused. "Do you understand what I'm telling you, Amanda?"

He stood up slowly, signifying their meeting was over. Amanda stood as well. Mr. Harvath then did something he'd never done with her before. He walked around his desk and held out his right hand to her. Amanda stared at it for a moment, then she moved the contract and books to her left hand. Mr. Harvath's grip was firm and cold, but, nonetheless, solid ... like bedrock.

"Good luck, Miss Walker. I want this done before Christmas."

Amanda forced a smile. "Absolutely, sir. I'll get it done, sir."

Her boss turned his back on her and walked over to the glass window to look outside. Amanda couldn't help but think, *It's like I'm not even in the room anymore.*

So she turned and walked out.

Wednesday, 9AM - 20,000 Feet above Pennsylvania

Amanda SAT COMFORTABLY IN FIRST CLASS ON Northern Airlines, flying from New York City to Detroit. From there, she'd have to catch a smaller plane to Marquette in Michigan's upper peninsula. She'd never been to Michigan before, let alone the upper peninsula. In her mind it had always been one of those out-of-the-way places that you needed a reason to go to or else what was the point. Michigan was almost in Canada and it was surrounded by water and covered in snow most of the year, so you had to be going there on purpose. And then she thought to herself *Why can't Sara Sinai live in California or Florida?*

She moved her glass of wine to one side and stared down at the clear, plastic envelope that her boss had given to her yesterday. She had plenty of time, so she reached down and opened it now. The more she read of the contract, the more she realized that this was going to be an easy author to land. Bedrock was offering her a multi-book deal, spread out over three years, complete with major marketing commitments, book tours, all the stuff that a self-published, previously unknown author would die for. And then she thought to herself, *Maybe I can wrap this up and be home tomorrow night in time for that Thanksgiving Day football party with my friends.*

She finished her wine and then held up her empty glass so the flight attendant could see. The woman smiled and nodded. She scurried away and came back a few seconds later to refill Amanda's wine glass.

"Thank you."

Amanda put the contract back in the clear, plastic folder and then pulled the legal-sized envelope out of her black, leather satchel. She opened it and read the background info on Sara Sinai. It was on letterhead from a detective agency in Paradise, Michigan.

> Subject's name - Sara Sinai
> Age - Unknown
> Gender - Female
> Appearance - Unknown
> Location - Keweenaw Peninsula, Michigan
> Address - Unknown
> Occupation - Independent Author
> Aliases - None discovered
> Known Acquaintances - None
> Marital Status - Unknown

> Summary: The name "Sara Sinai" appears to be an alias of some type, perhaps a pen name, as she is an author by trade. A thorough search of public records revealed no information. No marriages, no birth records, no business contracts, no paper trail of any kind. An online search revealed a limited online presence in the form of an Amazon Author page. A complete reading of all material posted by Sara Sinai reveals she resides in the upper peninsula of Michigan. References in her comments to places like the Bootjack Bar and Grill, the city of Houghton, copper mining, and the Keweenaw Waterway Upper Entrance Lighthouse all suggest she is located somewhere on the Keweenaw peninsula. Our recommendation is you begin your search in the township of Jackpine, located on the southern end of the peninsula an easy drive from Houghton.

> If this office can be of any further assistance, please contact us at your leisure. Please pay the attached invoice within 15 days.

Amanda wrinkled her brow and placed the paper back on her lap. Perhaps she wouldn't be home for Thanksgiving after all.

CHAPTER 3

"**W**ELL NOW THAT'S NOT WHAT I'm sayin,' Jack."

The man talking was old, probably just shy of a century by the looks of him, but ... age could be a deceptive thing up here in the wild and frozen north, what with wind-weathered faces, and time in general just seeming to melt from one year into the next. Chief of Police Jack Ruger let out a heavy sigh and tried one more time.

"So what exactly are you saying, Henry, because I have to write up an incident report here just in case this thing ends up going to the county prosecutor's desk."

The old man looked just as impatient with the chief as the chief looked with him.

"What I'm sayin' Jack, is I didn't see him 'xactly steal my chickens, but I know dern well it was him, cuz he hates me so much and he called me a crazy jack ass just last week!"

The chief of police smiled nervously and lowered his head to stare down at the snow. All around him it was speckled with bright, red chicken blood.

The wind was biting cold, but Jack, being born and raised here barely felt it. "Okay, Henry. I'll go talk to Tom about it and see if he can shed any light on this thing with your chickens." The younger man looked up sharply and made eye contact. "Sound fair enough, Henry?"

The older man looked off into the pine trees around him. They helped block the wind for his chicken coop, but the gale was howling now and blowing snow up in swirls that made him squint. But Henry didn't feel it. His cheeks had been frostbitten so many times that his skin was more like leather than skin. Finally, after what seemed like an eternity in the frozen cold, Henry nodded his head.

"Okay, Jack. I'll buy that. I know yer an honest man, even if ya are a cop."

The chief couldn't help but smile spontaneously at the last comment."Well thank you Henry." He reached out to shake the man's wrinkled and frail hand. Jack wore black gloves, but Henry's hands were bare and cold. They made eye contact one last time before Henry spit off into the snow just to the left of him.

"Okay, well, ya git back to me when ya find out who did it then."

And as Jack was walking away, Henry stopped him one more time. "Happy Thanksgiving, Jack."

Jack smiled and called over his shoulder. "You too, Henry. Don't eat too much turkey, tomorrow!"

The old man smiled, and said to himself under his breath after Jack was out of hearing. "We'll be a eatin' chicken this year. All five of 'em."

The chief of police walked back to his blue SUV and hopped inside. The engine was still running, and Jack quickly turned on the seat heater. The township of Jackpine had just purchased this new vehicle at his prompting and he was mighty grateful for it, especially with winter already biting down harder than a beaver on a birch tree. And winter in the upper peninsula was nothing to be trifled with. It was long and hard, and it seemed to last forever.

But ... Jack didn't seem to mind so much. Probably because he'd never really known anything different. He'd lived here most of his life, as did his foster parents, or, at least they had lived here until a terrible car accident about ten years ago. Jack still missed them.

Jack put the car in reverse and backed out to the main road. It was time to get some food.

Friday, 8:30AM - Jackpine Diner

"EXCUSE ME. I'M WONDERING IF YOU CAN HELP ME FIND someone?"

The lady behind the counter at the Jackpine Diner looked at Amanda as if she was from another world. "Wow! Yer not from around these parts are ya honey."

There were several other people in the small establishment, some of them were sipping coffee, while others were working on eggs, hash browns and toast. All of them were wearing camouflage clothing or large wool coats of red and black plaid.

Amanda was trying to be polite, but her patience was starting to wain. Her connecting flight in Detroit had been delayed, then cancelled with no idea when it might be rescheduled. The airline said there was very little demand for flights to Marquette and recommended she just rent a car and drive up. But Amanda wasn't an experienced driver, especially on the snow. In New York City she didn't even own a car, simply because public transportation and cabs were so prevalent, and where would you park even if you had a car? No, cars in New York City were mostly for the rich and famous and she was neither ... at least not yet.

So she'd taken an Indian Trails bus up I75 all the way to the Mackinaw Bridge and then across into the upper peninsula. She vowed to never do that again. She'd gotten nauseous about halfway into the drive and had lost her lunch at a rest stop in Grayling, where ever that was. But, at least she'd made it off the bus before puking. It had been so embarrassing as all the people on board had clapped and cheered for her while she heaved onto the snow-covered pavement. She had gone from her plush New York City office ... to first class plane fair and champagne ... to puking on a bus ride with farmers and factory workers. How far could she fall in just a few, short hours?

Michigan was a strange place. Riding across the bridge had scared her to death. Anchor to anchor it was about seven miles long, and the wind had pushed against the sides of the big bus, threatening to blow it off and into the icy water below. She'd never seen the great lakes before, but ... they seemed a lot like the Atlantic Ocean to her. Dark, foreboding, untamed and dangerous, especially with the weather so cold and the wind so strong.

At Marquette, on Thanksgiving morning, she'd rented a car and then got a motel room for the night. Then, after a hot shower, dinner and a good night's sleep, she had driven down US Highway 41 going west through towns like Negaunee, Ishpeming, Michigamme, Eagle Mills and then L'anse as she traveled north.

Seeing Lake Superior for the first time had been an eye-opener for her. It was huge ... massive, and so powerful and wild. And the severe cold and wind had shocked her. New York City could be very cold in the winter, but at least the buildings blocked the wind. Out here ... there was nothing to hold the wind at bay, so it slashed across the lake coming down from the Canadian north totally unchecked. She couldn't imagine anyone living any farther north than this.

Fortunately, the roads had been dry and the sun was out on that particular day, which, she was to learn later, was a rarity up here in the bowels of winter.

So now, Amanda, from the sophistication of the big city, now looked at Florence Wentley, a simple northwoods country girl from the backward town of Jackpine, and she couldn't for the life of her understand why a woman would stay here.

"No, I'm from New York City, and I'm trying to find a friend of mine."

Florence narrowed her eyes a bit. "Really, honey. You're from the big apple and you came all the way here to visit someone in Jackpine? I don't think so."

Florence was the owner of the Jackpine Diner, and pretty much always said what she was thinking. For the people of Jackpine, it was normal, because lots of country people are like that. But it was new to Amanda, so she hesitated before answering. "Are you calling me a liar?"

Florence didn't miss a beat. "If the shoe fits, honey."

Amanda started to get mad, but managed to control herself, just barely. Florence laughed and broke the tension.

"Who ya lookin' for honey?"

Amanda was deep in the process of trying to figure out why this stranger kept calling her 'honey' but Florence took control. "You want somethin' to drink, honey? You look like ya had a rough day."

Amanda let out a sigh. She didn't understand these northern woods people, but at least this was a start, and she had to find Sara Sinai.

"Why thank you. It's very cold outside and I could use a nice, hot espresso, with two shots, a dash of soy and light on the whip, please."

Florence laughed out loud. The man seated at the counter two chairs over laughed as well. All his tobacco-stained teeth showed as he did, causing Amanda to grimace involuntarily.

"Sure thing, honey."

Florence flipped over a coffee mug and reached to her left for a coffee pot. She filled the mug quickly, without even looking at it, as if she'd done it a million times, then she reached under the counter and pulled out a bottle of Jack Daniels whiskey and poured in two shots. After that she replaced the whiskey under the counter and pulled up a can of whipped cream and gave it one, short squirt.

"There ya go, honey. Now who ya lookin' for?"

Amanda looked down at the coffee mug in disbelief. Was she supposed to drink this? She slowly reached down to pick it up. The cup was steaming hot, and the warm glass mug felt so good on her ice-cold hands. She raised it to her mouth and smelled the combination of coffee, cream and alcohol. It seemed to have a settling effect on her.

"This smells good."

Florence smiled, and Amanda noticed that one of her upper teeth was missing on the right side. She couldn't help but stare at it. "Taste it, honey. Ya have to actually drink it to get the full effect."

So Amanda took a tiny sip. The hot liquid clawed its way down her throat and into her stomach, warming everything that it touched. She smiled, and then took another sip.

"It's good."

Florence nodded, but said nothing. The man two seats down spoke. "Can I get one of those fer me too, Flo?"

Florence gave him a look cold enough to freeze skin on contact. "Shut the hell up, Paul. You just got out of the clink for drunk and disorderly. Jack would kill me if I gave you a drink."

The sixty-five-year-old man turned back to his eggs and hash browns without comment. Florence looked back to Amanda. "So who ya lookin' for?"

Amanda took another small sip before answering. "Her name is Sara Sinai."

A blank look came over Flo's face, and then she became thoughtful, then blank again. Finally she answered. "Nope."

Amanda waited for more, but apparently that was the extent of her answer. "Excuse me?"

"Nope. Ain't nobody by that name here."

Amanda looked around the room and then back at Florence. "Are you sure, because I was told she lives here?"

Paul from two stools down piped up again. "Nope. That lady don't live here. I been in Jackpine my whole life, 'n never heard a such a name. That's a stupid name."

Florence cut him off. "Shut up, Paul er I'll drop kick yer butt out that door. Don't be rude to visitors, even if they are from New York City."

Paul shut up and went back to the last of his hash browns.

Just then the door of the diner opened up, clanging the bell over the door and a gush of icy wind blew in, followed quickly by a man in his mid-thirties. He was wearing flannel-lined blue jeans, with the cuffs turned up about three inches at the bottom, black lace-up leather boots, and a grey sweat shirt.

Florence beamed as he walked through the door. "Mornin', chief! You want the usual?"

The man was tall, about six-three, with a muscular build. He had short, dark brown hair with a little curl to the ends, especially up front. "Yeah, thanks Flo."

Amanda caught herself staring at him. There was something about him that seemed different than the other people she'd met here so far. He seemed ... out of place, an anomaly, like the embodiment of a strong and polite sophistication. She knew that instinctively from his first three words and by the way he carried himself.

"Havin' a good day, Jack?"

Jack nodded. "You bet Flo. Every day's good in Jackpine." And then he turned to the man eating his hash browns. "You have a good Thanksgiving, Paul?"

Paul nodded. "Yeah, but I can't talk about it er Flo's gonna kick me out."

Jack laughed out loud, and then he looked over at Amanda for the first time. He gave her a glance that lasted just a mite over a half second, then he turned back to Flo. "So what about you, Flo? You get to see those grand kids of yours?"

Flo smiled as she poured coffee into a large, styrofoam cup. Then she put a plastic lid on it. "Yep. Sure did. Cooked a big old turkey, with stuffing, pumpkin pie 'n all the fixin's. Lots a mashed potatoes 'n gravy too."

Jack smiled. His teeth were white and straight and perfect. Amanda forced herself to look away for a moment.

"That's good, Flo. I love those little ones of yours. They're good people."

He reached over and took the coffee from Florence. "Thank you, Flo." And then he turned and headed for the door. The door opened and the wind rushed in again. He turned as he was leaving.

"You stay off the sauce, Paul."

Paul didn't turn around, he just raised his left hand and gave it a jiggle. "Never touch the stuff, chief."

And then he was gone, the echo of the door bell fading, into the cloudy, upper peninsula morning.

Flo looked back at Amanda. "God if I was twenty years younger and better lookin'.''

And then Paul chimed in. "But ya ain't, so ya can't, so just stop yappin' 'bout it."

Florence was getting ready to snap back at him, but Amanda broke in quickly. "Who was that guy?"

"Oh, that's just the chief."

Amanda took another sip of her coffee. "The chief?"

Florence took a wet rag out from the sink behind her and wiped a few crumbs off into her hand, where she then threw them into the trash beside her.

"Yep. That's Jack, the chief of police."

Amanda turned and looked out the big, plate glass window of the diner as he drove away in his blue SUV. "He wasn't wearing a uniform."

Flo shrugged. "He don't need to. We all know who he is and what he does."

Amanda nodded and pulled her coat a little tighter to her body. Every time the door opened it got a little colder inside. "So how many police do you have in Jackpine?"

Flo turned and walked over to Paul. "Ya want anything else, there, Paul?" But the old man shook his head.

"Nah. I best be headin' back to the house." And he dropped a five-dollar bill on the counter and walked toward the door. Flo took his plate and silverware and moved it over to the sink. Then she turned back to Amanda.

"So what's yer name there, honey?"

Out of habit, Amanda placed her mug on the counter and reached into her satchel and pulled out a business card. She handed it to Flo, who looked at it and then squinted her eyes. "Bedrock publishing. I heard of 'em."

And then she continued talking as if the fancy business card meant nothing. "We just have the one."

Amanda looked confused. "The one?"

Florence looked at Amanda as if she were slow-witted. "Yes, honey. One. One cop. You asked how many cops we got here in Jackpine. Just the one."

Amanda looked down at her coffee mug. To her surprise it was almost gone. "Well, it's a small town. I guess one cop should be enough." She waited a moment, taking one final drink from her mug. "So how many people live in Jackpine?"

Flo shrugged. "Don't know."

"You don't know how many people in your own town?"

"Nope."

"That seems odd."

"No it don't. I bet you don't know how many live in New York City."

Amanda thought about it for a moment. Come to think of it, she didn't know how many people lived in New York. And then Flo walked over to clean the counter where Paul had been sitting. "You just missed the mayor or you coulda asked him. I bet he'd know."

"Jack is the mayor as well?"

Florence just looked at her like she was daft and shook her head from side to side. "No, honey. Paul. Jack's the chief of police. I done told ya that already."

"Paul is the mayor?" Flo didn't answer. "Seems like having an alcoholic mayor might not be such a good idea."

Florence stopped cleaning and looked at Amanda. "Listen, sweetheart. We kin be good friends so don't screw it up. Don't come into Jackpine 'n try 'n tell us how to run the town. Seems like New York City ain't all that great ya know."

Amanda started to answer, but then stopped herself. She wanted to get along with this woman. "I see what you mean."

And then she set her coffee mug down on the counter. "So,

where do you think I should start looking for my friend?"

Florence looked thoughtfully around the diner nd then back at Amanda. "Well, honey. I guess, if'n it was me. I'd go ask the chief."

"You mean Jack?"

Flo nodded. "Who else would I mean? I done told ya we only got one cop here."

Amanda didn't want to get tangled up in a circular conversation again, so she just nodded. "I see. So where can I find the chief right now?"

Florence pointed with her left hand out the window. "Just follow the road down that way until ya come to the red, brick building. It's the township hall. Got the police, the ambulance and the fire truck all in one building. It was a lot cheaper to build it that way. You'll see the chief's SUV right out front."

Amanda smiled. "Thank you Florence. You've been a great help. How much for the coffee?"

And then Florence smiled again. "That wasn't coffee, dear. That was hot espresso, with two shots, a dash of soy and light on the whip."

Amanda couldn't help but smile. The Jack Daniels had loosened her up a bit. She opened her billfold and pulled out her Bedrock Publishing credit card and extended it out to Flo. But Florence just shook her head. "Sorry, honey. Don't you got no cash?"

Amanda looked flustered. "Why ... no. I ... seldom carry cash with me."

The older woman flashed a smile, highlighting her missing tooth. "Well, I seldom take credit cards. It's on the house, honey. Welcome to Jackpine."

And then she reached under the counter and pulled out a brown grocery bag with the top stapled shut. "Just do me a favor, will ya?"

Amanda nodded hesitantly. "Okay ..."

"Just give this bag to Jack. It's leftovers from Thanksgiving dinner, and I forgot to give it to him when he was in here."

Amanda nodded and reached out to take the bag. "Okay. Guess I can do that."

And then Florence turned and walked back into the kitchen to yell at the hired help.

Amanda looked around at the few other customers inside the diner. They looked back at her but said nothing. She put her card back into her pocketbook and stood to leave. Here she was, in Jackpine, Michigan, about as far from civilization as she could possibly get without falling off the edge of the world. She wanted to turn around and head back to the safety of New York City, but ... then she recalled Mr. Harvath's word of warning to her.

> "This client will make or break your career in the publishing industry, Miss Walker. Do you understand what I'm telling you?"

And then she thought to herself as the bell over the door clanged out and the ice-cold wind blew into her collar, freezing her neck. *Yes, Mr. Harvath. I understand. I'm trapped in an ice-cold hell until I can find Sara Sinai, a woman who appears to not exist. Then I have to sign her up for the team and only then will I be allowed to come back to the real world. Until then ... I'm trapped here in the whacky world of Jackpine.*

CHAPTER 4

AMANDA PULLED HER COLLAR UP as far as she could get it, but it was still insufficient to ward off the cold. The sun was still shining, but she couldn't feel any warmth from it. Her coat was definitely better suited to the high fashion of New York City than it was the wilds of upper Michigan. She was not prepared for this assignment ... either emotionally or physically.

She walked up to the gray, steel door with a sheet of glass on the top half with the words "Jackpine Township Police Department" inscribed in the form of a plastic decal. She frowned ... not very professional. She opened the door and walked in.

"Just tell me straight out, Tom. Did you or did you not shoot the man's chickens?"

There was silence as Jack Ruger listened to the reply. He looked up briefly from the phone just long enough to see Amanda's presence. "You didn't answer my question, Tom. Last time you avoided my questions you were lying to me."

More silence as Tom replied. "Well I don't care if he did call you a dirty name. That's not the way we act here in Jackpine. Now I'll go ahead and remind Henry how important it is to speak to his neighbor's with respect, but you have to replace the chickens, all five of them. Do you understand?"

Jack swiveled in his office chair and put his back to Amanda for a few seconds. Then he came back around again, and he resumed talking. "I know, Tom. You two have been friends since kindergarten and he hurt your feelings, but ..." Amanda couldn't help but eavesdrop on the conversation. It seemed so unusual for a cop to be acting this way. "Listen, Tom. Just go get it done and return peace to Jackpine, okay?"

Jack nodded. "That's right. Now I'll be following up on it too, so make sure you get it done today."

He made eye contact with Amanda for the first time. "That's right, Tom. Thank you. I appreciate you too. Tell the misses I said hello."

And then he hung up and spoke his first words to Amanda Walker. "How may I help you, Ma'am?"

She smiled. "May I sit down?"

"Well, yes, of course. I'm sorry, I forgot my manners for a second." He got up from his chair and walked around the desk to Amanda. He unfolded a chair that was leaning against the ugly, green painted wall and set it on the floor and held it while she sat down.

"Just dealing with an emergency."

Amanda smiled again. "Yes, that sounded very important."

Jack walked back to his desk and sat down on the corner of it. Amanda couldn't help but notice the muscles in his thighs, even through the blue denim pants. And then he reached out his right hand. "My name's Jack Ruger. I'm the chief of police here in Jackpine."

Amanda quickly shook his outstretched hand. Right away she noticed how strong and warm it was. It wasn't like her boss, Mr. Harvath, at all. Then she pulled out her pocketbook and removed another business card. Jack took it with his left hand and looked down at it. Then he turned it over in his hand. "That's a very nice business card, Ms. Walker."

She nodded. "Why thank you, Chief Ruger."

"Please, call me Jack. Everyone else around here does."

"Of course. Please call me Amanda."

24

There was a moment of clumsy silence. Finally, Jack spoke up. "So what brings you to Jackpine, Amanda?"

Amanda crossed her legs, all the while maintaining eye contact with him to see if he would glance down at her figure. She was a bit disappointed when his eyes remained focused on her face.

"Well, I'm looking for a friend."

Jack nodded. "And the friend's name is ...?"

"Sinai, Sara Sinai."

Amanda thought she saw a slight change in his posture, some hint of perhaps recognition, but she couldn't be sure. Maybe she was just imagining it. But there was something definitely there that she couldn't quite read.

"Well, do you have an address?"

"No. I'm afraid not. I accidently deleted it from my contacts."

Jack's eyes narrowed. "So you came all the way to Jackpine from New York City to visit a friend without the address?" Jack cocked his head to the left just a little. "Well, now, Ma'am, now you'll excuse me if I think that's a bit peculiar."

Amanda looked down at her lap. She was accustomed to feeling in charge of most conversations, but ... Jack Ruger ... he seemed to have a presence that belied the control of others. She didn't say anything.

"So, Ms. Walker, what can you tell me about your friend. I'd loved to help you, but I need a little bit to go on."

Amanda squirmed in the folding chair. She knew very little about Sara Sinai, but how could she tell that to him now, especially after claiming to be her friend? And then she remembered the books.

"My friend is an author. She wrote these three books."

And she reached into her black. leather satchel beside her on the floor and handed them to the police officer.

Jack took them, and read the titles, and then turned them over to peruse the back covers. "So your friend Sara is a romance writer." And then he held up the top book with the front cover facing out. "So is this one any good?"

Amanda's heart stopped. She hadn't taken the time to read any of the books yet, so she honestly didn't know. "Umm, well ... Yes. Of course. Sara is an awesome writer. All her books are good. They're best sellers on Amazon."

Jack smiled softly. "Well, I'm sure she'll be happy to hear that from your own mouth when you finally do locate her."

And then he turned his head and looked out the window. The sun was streaming in, but then it suddenly stopped, as if a light switch had been flicked off. The winter outside blew snow against the window glass.

"Well, Amanda, I'm going to be honest with you, which, I'm sorry to say, is more than you've done for me. You see, here in Jackpine we appreciate candor, and people who pretend to be something that they're not, well ... let's just say we don't value that."

Amanda pretended to be offended. "You don't believe me?"

Jack shook his head from side to side. "No, Ms. Walker. Not even for a second." Amanda squirmed in her chair. "Now, sure I believe you're from New York and that you work for Bedrock Publishing, like your business card says, but ... as far as you being good friends with Sara Sinai ... I don't think you even know the woman."

And then Jack Ruger smiled, totally disarming Amanda, so much so that she came to an unusual decision, one that would never work in New York City.

"Mr. Ruger ... I apologize. I've been misleading you about that. But I wonder if, perhaps, just maybe ... you could give me another chance?"

Jack laughed out loud, and his laughter was even more disarming than his smile.

"Sure thing. Not a problem. I guess we all make mistakes from time to time." And then he stood up and moved around his desk and sat down in his chair. "Go ahead, Amanda. Tell me the truth."

Amanda let out a huge sigh, relaxed for a moment and then launched into her explanation. "Okay, well, here it is then. I'm an editor from New York City, like my business card says, and my boss sent me here to offer Sara Sinai a publishing contract. I just need to find her so I can get this wrapped up and get back to my office. Normally we do this kind of thing over the phone, or email or even snail mail, but ... Ms. Sinai doesn't appear to have much of an online presence, and we frankly don't know where to find her."

Jack nodded. "So how did you know she was here in Jackpine?"

"We don't know for sure. It's just that the ... well ..." She reached into her satchel and brought out the private detective's report and handed it to him. He took it and read it to himself. Amanda waited impatiently. It was taking him a long time to read it. She waited as long as she could before interrupting his thoughts.

"So, Mr. Ruger, what do you think?"

He handed the report back to her and sighed. "I think you're between a rock and hard place. I don't know of anyone in the whole Keweenaw peninsula, let alone Jackpine who is named Sara Sinai. I think it's probably like the private eye said; that's her pen name." And then he looked her in the eyes. "Ms. Walker, is it possible that Ms. Sinai doesn't want to be found by you or by anyone else?"

Amanda looked down at her empty lap. "Oh, I suppose. But if she just knew how much money we're offering her, then I know she'd want to meet with me. This is a really good offer here. We're talking about major marketing, a nationwide book tour, TV and radio interviews. This could change the author's life forever. She'll be famous!"

Jack leaned back in his office chair and it squeaked a bit. He leaned forward again and his dark-brown eyes got real serious. "Ms. Walker, people don't move to Jackpine because they want to be famous or rich or on television. They move to

Jackpine to get away from all those things."

Amanda glanced out the window at the snow swirling up against the glass. "So ... are you saying that you know Sara and that she doesn't want to talk to me?"

Jack moved his hands up to the top of his desk, and he interlaced his fingers there on the artificial top. "No, Ma'am, that's not exactly what I'm saying. But here's what I'll do." And he moved his folded hands from the desk and onto his chest. "I'll start asking around the township and see if anyone knows anyone new around here. If I find Sara, then I'll see if she wants to talk to you. And ... if she does, I've got your cell number here, I'll just give you a call."

Amanda thought about that for a moment. She didn't like waiting. "Well, I appreciate your help, but ... what if I want to look around myself, you know, ask people on my own?"

Jack unclasped his hands and stood up from his chair. "Not a problem. This is America, and you're free to talk to anyone you like. But ... let me give you some advice first."

Amanda nodded. "Okay, what is it?"

Jack walked around his desk and stood in front of her, just a few feet away. His smell had the hint of a sweet and spicy pine tree. "People here in Jackpine like peace and quiet, and I get paid to keep it that way, so please, don't get people all riled up about this thing. Just be discreet, go easy, and I can probably find out for you what you need to know."

Amanda nodded and then stood to her feet as well. That's when she noticed how tall the chief was. Amanda was five foot eight, but the chief was still quite a bit taller than her.

"So you'll call me as soon as you know anything?"

Jack nodded. "I'll get started right away and then call you tonight."

Amanda bent down to retrieve her satchel. "Oh, you might have trouble getting through to me on the first try, because my cell phone hasn't been working very well since I crossed the Mackinaw bridge."

He smiled. "I know. It happens to everyone. It's part of the ambience up here. Tons of snow, sub-zero temperatures, and bad cell coverage. You'll get used to it."

Deep inside, Amanda countered his assertion. *No way will I ever get used to living like this. I won't be here long enough.* And then she turned and walked toward the door. "Oh, by the way ... I didn't see a motel here in town. Where can I get a room?"

Jack moved forward and held the door open for her. "Head back down 41 through Baraga to L'Anse. And make sure you check out the Hilltop Bakery while you're there. The cinnamon rolls are incredible. You'll gain weight just looking at them."

She gave him a confused look. "Why would I want to gain weight?"

And Jack smiled as a rush of bitter, icy wind pushed into his office. "That means they taste good, Ms. Walker."

So Amanda walked out the door, pulling up her collar, trying desperately and vainly to keep the cold wind off her neck. Jack closed the door behind her and stared at her back as she walked to her car.

And then he walked back to his desk and sat in his chair, shaking his head from side to side. "These New York people have no idea which end of the barrel the round comes out of."

And then he looked back down at his desk and tried to figure out what he should do next.

CHAPTER 5

AMANDA PULLED HER COLLAR UP as far as she could and walked to her car. It wasn't the car she'd wanted to rent, but on Thanksgiving day in Marquette, she'd been lucky to get this one. It was a Mitzubishi Mirage, just a tiny four-door compact that didn't seem to handle well in the snow and ice. She also had trouble getting the heater to warm up in all this cold.

She pulled her bare hand out of her coat pocket and reached down to open the door, but it wouldn't budge. She pulled again and again, but it had frozen shut. Amanda put her hand back in her pocket and hugged herself with her arms. Going back inside and asking for help was out of the question. Her pride wouldn't allow her to do that, so she would just have to figure it out for herself. Amanda thought for a moment and then pushed at the door with her hip before trying to open it again. It didn't work, so she slammed her body up against the car even harder. Still nothing. She tried it several more times with the same result.

The wind was pouring down under her collar now, and she wished she had a furry parka with a hood like she'd seen eskimos wear on television. Amanda looked down main street towards the diner, but it seemed like a long way to walk in this cold. She was just about to begin the long, cold trek when a

30

voice startled her.

"Can I help you, Amanda?"

She jumped back a step at the sound of Jack's voice, but quickly recovered her composure. "Oh, no. I'm fine. I'm just waiting."

Jack Ruger was wearing no coat. He'd left it inside, but didn't seem to be affected by the wind and the cold. He smiled again, and it drove her crazy. "It's just that I saw you from the window, you know, throwing your body against the car and wondered if you might be having trouble getting it open."

Amanda forced a fake smile onto her face and finally nodded in admission. "Okay, yes. I was having a little trouble with it."

Jack stepped forward and grasped the handle with his right hand and gave it a hard pull. It quickly opened. "Sometimes they get frozen shut up here. It happens quite a bit actually. Especially with these smaller cars for some reason."

He held the door for her as she stepped inside and sat down. That's when she saw the bag of food she'd promised Forence that she'd deliver. She started the car and rolled down the window. "This is from Florence. She asked me to give it to you."

Jack smiled and reached out to take it with his left hand. "Why, thank you ma'am. I appreciate it." She started to roll the window back up, but he spoke again, prompting her to stop. "Be careful in this little car. They don't handle too well on icy roads and in deep snow. You might want to trade it in for an SUV while you're up here."

She nodded her thanks and started rolling the window up again, but he still wasn't finished. "There's a nasty storm front moving in, so you shouldn't dawdle too long here in Jackpine. You might want to head straight on down to L'Anse to the motel until the storm blows over."

"Thank you Chief Ruger. I appreciate your concern, but I want to ask a few questions first."

Jack nodded, the wind blowing his coarse, brown hair in

the growing gale. "Suit yourself then."

AMANDA DROVE AWAY, LEAVING THE CHIEF OF POLICE standing alone in the cold. He waved but she didn't return the gesture. A few minutes later she parked back at the diner and walked in through the door. The ever-diligent bell rang announcing her arrival. Florence was behind the counter and she looked up and smiled softly. Amanda couldn't help but wonder to herself *Why is everyone so happy up here?*

"So did you find the chief okay?"

Amanda walked up and sat down on a bar stool. "Yes, I found him. He said he'd ask around and get back to me, but nothing definite."

It was already 10:30AM on her first day in Jackpine and already she knew nothing more than when she'd left New York City. She moved the leather satchel up onto the counter and pulled out the three paperback romance novels. She laid two of them on the counter and opened one of them to read.

"Can I get you something to eat while you read?"

Amanda was never much of a breakfast eater, but she didn't want to take up the seat without ordering something. "Sure. What do you recommend, Florence?"

Florence wiped her hands on her apron and nodded. "You look like a light eater. How about some bacon and eggs to get you fattened up."

Amanda didn't understand this woman. Why would anyone want to be fattened up? She thought about it for a minute. *Should she ask for her usual breakfast? Would Florence even know what it was?* She decided to give it a try.

"Usually I have the egg-white omelette, made with coconut milk, no meat please. Just add some diced red peppers, chives, a little fresh garlic, cracked black pepper and some pink Himalayan salt."

Florence didn't bat an eye. She simply turned and walked back to the kitchen. "Comin' right up. sweetheart."

Amanda smiled and thought quietly. *Wow! That was easy.*

Maybe I judged her too harshly. Perhaps there was more civilization up here than she'd first thought. Amanda appeared to be alone in the dining area now. She'd meant to ask around, but everyone was gone now. She picked up the first paperback book and turned it over in her hand. Amazon printers did a great job at mass-market printing, but they skimped at every turn, using the cheapest paper and ink but their processes were streamlined and efficient. Obviously that was a business model that worked for them financially, but still, Amanda liked a thicker paper, something that she could hold onto and crinkle if she wanted to. She liked to smell the ink of a fresh print run, and she liked her paperback covers with thick card stock instead of the flimsy covers that never held up to the test of time. That's one thing she'd always liked about Bedrock Publishing: they did a first-rate production job, using nothing but the best material, and their layout and design was first-rate, never cutting corners. Bedrock Publishing prided themselves in making a quality product that competed with any book on the market.

She opened the book cover and scanned over the copyright page. Nothing unusual there. She stopped short at the dedication page.

To purity and old-fashioned romance.
To those who remember.

Amanda furled her brow. What was that all about? Purity? In a romance novel? That didn't make any sense. That was a terrible marketing scheme. All the best sellers were laced with decadence, wild passion, and steamy bedroom scenes. There must be a catch. So she read the first chapter while waiting for her omelette. It was a very quick read. The words seemed to flow off the page, as if they wanted to be read, as if the writer had some special knack for crafting sentences that others did not.

She finished just as Florence walked up and placed the

thick and heavy white, glass platter in front of her. Her omelette was floating in bacon grease, like the scum on a farm
pond in the heat of summer. There were four strips of bacon
and four sausage links off to the side as well. Amanda looked
down at it, and then back up helplessly at Florence. She slowly closed the novel and placed it off to one side.

"You gave me bacon and sausage."

Florence smiled. "Yeah, I know. Ya didn't ask for it, but I
figured, what the heck, yer new in town so I won't charge ya
for the meat. 'Sides, ya don't got any money anyways."

Amanda looked down at the island of meat and eggs, surrounded by waves of hot grease, lapping against the shoreline
on her plate. She was stupefied. Florence was still smiling, as
if expecting to be thanked for her efforts. In New York City,
she would have scolded the waitress and demanded she be
fired. But here ... in Jackpine ... she was pushing up against
the boundaries of normalcy. In the end, she took the high road.

"Thank you, Florence. That's very sweet of you."

And then she picked up her fork, but Florence interrupted
her. "Aren't you going to pray first?"

Amanda looked up. "What?"

Florence laughed out loud and reached over to take
Amanda's hand. It caught her so far off guard that she didn't
have the presence of mind to be offended and pull away.

"It's okay I got this one."

And then Florence closed her eyes and bowed her head,
all the while holding Amanda's hand in both of her own. She
squeezed loosely.

"Dear Lord, thank you for this good food, for the warmth,
and for our new friend, Amanda. Amen."

And then Florence turned and walked away, leaving
Amanda by herself totally stupefied. No one had ever prayed
with her before. Amanda looked down again at the plate before her. *What was she supposed to do with all this food?* She
sighed quietly and resolved herself to make the best of a bad
situation. After all, she'd once been sent on assignment to

the Panama Canal zone and been forced to eat monkey meat. Afterwards, she'd thrown up at the hotel, but, the important thing was, she'd signed the author and been promoted in the process. Amanda took a deep breath. *You can do this, girl!*

She scooped up a small piece of omelette on her fork and placed it on the tip of her tongue, expecting the worst. Instead, her taste buds were overwhelmed with flavor. She accepted the bite and began to chew. Unprecedented things happened to her mouth. First, there was a bit of euphoria, then a burst of garlic flavor, right before ... her mouth began to go numb. And she began to feel the heat; it was latent at first, but when it kicked in, it was like the afterburners on an F18 Superhornet fighter jet.

At first it was painful, but then, as the numbness infiltrated her mouth, the pain subsided, allowing her to take another bite. Amanda paused long enough to take a brief look around the diner. She took another bite, and then another and another. Five minutes later she looked down at her plate and was surprised to see the omelette was gone. Amanda looked up and basked in the heat that still spread from her mouth all the way down into her stomach. Amanda was amazed. That was the best-tasting omelette of her life.

Involuntarily, she reached her left hand up to wipe her brow, only to discover it was beaded with perspiration. That surprised her, but not as much as the light-headedness that followed. She grabbed the counter with her right hand to keep from falling off the bar stool, but the dizziness quickly passed. Amanda looked down at the sausage and bacon, wondering ... *should I try them too?* She cut one of the sausage links in quarters and lifted the meat gingerly to her mouth. She tasted it and nodded her head up and down, all the while, wondering, *why do I like this? I hate meat.*

She quickly ate the sausage, and then started on the bacon. It was good too and was soon gone. Amanda looked down at the empty plate. A part of her was disappointed to see the food gone, but then she noticed the bloating in her stomach and the overfull feeling was almost overwhelming to her. Perhaps ... she'd eaten too much? And that's when the euphoria overtook her, and she fell off the bar stool, onto the tile floor, hitting her head with a resounding crack!

CHAPTER 6

<u>*Saturday, 8AM - Baraga County Memorial Hospital*</u>

AMANDA WOKE UP THE NEXT MORNing. lying in a hospital bed. Her eyes fluttered for a moment, then the bright light hit and she quickly closed them again. *Why did her head hurt so much?* She heard voices in the room, but they seemed so far away and fuzzy, like they were coming from another world, traveling across billions of miles before landing on her brain and jackhammering their way into her skull. If she concentrated, she could barely make out the words.

"Well, it's not like I done it on purpose, Jack! I just got the hot peppers mixed up that's all. I thought they was the regular cayennes, but they was the Carolina Reapers."

Through the fog in her head, she heard Jack whistle softly. "Oh come on, Flo, not the Reapers! Those are the hottest peppers on the planet."

"I know, Jack. I already threw 'em away. I just bought 'em cuz I thought they was cool."

Amanda was starting to hear things more clearly now, and she thought to herself. *No, they're definitely not cool.*

"Well, we'll be lucky if she doesn't sue us for this. That's what people from New York City do, you know. They wait for something bad to happen to them, and then they hire a lawyer and take their neighbors to court. You could lose your diner over this, Flo."

Florence started to cry. Amanda opened her brown eyes just a tiny slit, enough to see what was going on. Her eyes slowly adjusted to the light, and she saw Jack holding Florence, trying to comfort her.

"It's okay, Flo. We'll work it out somehow. Maybe she's not like other New York City folks."

"I'm not."

When Florence heard Amanda's voice, she glanced over and interrupted her tears. Then she pushed Jack away and walked over to the bed to stand beside Amanda.

"Honey, I am so sorry. I didn't mean to poison you. I just got the peppers all mixed up. Ya gotta believe me."

Amanda tried to smile, but it hurt too bad. "I know, Florence. Don't worry about it." She paused. "Why does my head hurt so bad? Is that from the chili peppers?"

Florence wiped away a tear with her left hand. "No, honey. You hit yer head on the tile floor when ya fell off the stool. The doc says ya got a mild concussion. That's why ya was pukin' all over the place."

Jack stood off in the background, letting the scene play out, just watching and taking it all in.

"I puked in your diner?"

Florence nodded. "That's puttin' it mildly sweetheart. I don't think I ever saw nobody puke more 'n that in my whole life. It was one fer the record books."

Amanda glanced over at Jack without turning her head. It hurt to move her neck. For some reason she hoped that Jack hadn't seen her mess.

"I'm really sorry, Flo. I didn't mean to mess up your restaurant. It's just ... I don't think I've ever tasted anything so good in my whole life."

Florence reached down to stroke Amanda's cheek with her fingers. It struck Amanda as motherly, and she was touched by it. Her own parents lived in California, and she'd had very little contact with them since moving to New York. And, even when she'd been a child, there had been very little physical affection in her family.

"Will I be okay?"

That's when Jack moved forward and stood on the other side of the bed. "The doctor says you'll be fine. You just need a few days of bed rest and observation. After that you should be able to move around and gradually return to normal."

Amanda smelled Jack now from just a few feet away. It was that sweet pine scent again, and it was a welcome change to the disinfectant aroma that all hospitals had. She didn't know why, but she really liked Jack's scent. She'd never smelled anything like it before, either in New York or California. Jack was wearing a heavy, flannel shirt; it looked like it was lined with some kind of fleece. Amanda found herself wanting to reach out and touch it.

She noticed the gold badge, in the shape of a shield hanging on Jack's heavy, black, leather belt. And there was a gun on his right hip as well. For some reason she hadn't noticed it before.

"Is that a real gun?"

Jack didn't answer her. Instead, he looked over at Florence before speaking. "Flo, don't you think you ought to be getting back to the diner? It's after 10AM and Paul's going to be starved by now. You know the man can't cook for himself."

Florence laughed out loud. "You got that right. That man is helpless as they come."

And then she looked down again, directly into Amanda's eyes as she caressed her cheek. Then she moved a lock of hair away from Amanda's right eye.

"I love yer hair, sweetie. Wish I had hair like that."

Amanda smiled involuntarily. "Thank you."

And then, for the second time in as many days, Florence did something very strange to Amanda. She moved her left hand up to Amanda's forehead, brushed away the hair, and then began to pray.

"Dear God. Please heal this little girl. Touch her head and

make it all better. We thank ya in advance."

And then she bent down and kissed Amanda's forehead, picked her purse up off the chair beside the bed, and she was gone.

Jack watched her go and then turned back to face Amanda. He didn't say anything at first, and the silence was clumsy. Then he pointed over to the chair in the corner.

"Do you mind if I sit down so we can talk?"

Amanda nodded her head and immediately regretted it. The pain shot through her skull, and a wave of sudden nausea rushed over her. She closed her eyes and thought for a moment. She had to stop moving.

"That's fine, chief."

Jack retrieved the chair and sat down to the right of her hospital bed. He turned the back of the chair away from himself and straddled it with his forearms resting on the top of the chair back. He looked too serious for Amanda, and it made her feel uncomfortable.

"Is something wrong?"

Jack smiled softly. "You mean is something wrong aside from the fact that you almost died and you're laying in a hospital bed thousands of miles from your home in a strange place?"

Amanda closed her eyes and returned his smile. "Well ... I guess it sounds worse when you put it that way. I almost died?"

Jack nodded. "You were lying face down in a pool of vomit and your airway was clogged. We had to perform CPR for a while to get you stabilized."

She looked directly into his blue eyes, searching for some hint of revulsion, but she saw none. "We? Do you mean you?"

Jack looked down at the tile floor and laughed softly. "Yeah, I suppose it was me for the first 15 minutes until the EMTs could get there. They took over after that."

Amanda slowly turned her head away, braving the pain she knew would come. "So ... you ... put your mouth on my ..."

Jack nodded. "Yes, Ma'am. But it was all in the line of duty, I assure you."

Amanda felt the blood rise to her face as it flushed. "Oh, that must have been terrible, with all that puke and stuff. Jack, I am so sorry." And then she grew silent. Jack didn't say a word ... he just waited.

"So ... it sounds like you saved my life."

Jack nodded. "I reckon I did."

Amanda looked into his face. She saw no judgement, no revulsion, no hint of negativity. And then she smiled as much as the pain would allow.

"Thank you, Jack. I owe you."

Jack looked down at the tile, then back up again. "Don't mention it. I just don't want you getting the wrong idea."

Amanda reached up with her left hand and fidgeted with the white bed sheet. "The wrong idea? What do you mean?"

And then she thought she saw him almost blush. "Well, Amanda, I don't usually kiss a woman on the first date, especially not one covered in vomit and drool."

She laughed softly, but quickly mastered herself to relieve the pain. "I'd hardly call that a date, Chief Ruger." And then she thought for a moment. "Although ... if it had been a date, I certainly would rank it up there with my top three worst dates of all time."

Jack laughed out loud, and the huskiness of his voice brought shivers to Amanda's body. He was probably the most masculine man she'd ever met. He was just so different from the men in New York City. She couldn't quite put her finger on it, but ... she found his polite manner, his eyes, the way they seemed to smile at her, his broad shoulders and his muscular chest and arms overwhelming. He was like a Christmas package she'd never unwrapped before. And she wondered ...

"Well, Miss Walker, perhaps we should remedy that. I can't have you leaving Jackpine knowing that I was one of your worst dates ever."

And then he looked over at the wall. Amanda didn't know

what he was thinking, and it made her nervous. Inside his head, Jack was nervous too, so he followed the wires and tubes attached to the wall with his eyes. It was like connecting the dots, and it helped him focus.

"As soon as we can spring you from this place, I'd like to show you a little yooper hospitality. Perhaps take you to dinner in the big city?"

Her heart fluttered. "Are you asking me on a date? A formal date?"

Amanda couldn't believe her ears. First, he'd caught her lying to him, and then he'd seen her facedown in a puddle of her own puke. He'd even tasted her vomit. And now ... he was asking her out?

"Yes, Ma'am. I'm asking you on a date ... a proper date, one without puke and drool and carolina reapers."

This type of thing had never happened to her before. Usually a man just wanted her for what he could get out of her, and, quite frankly, her motives had seldom been sincere either. Dating in New York City had always been a game, like a selfish dance, but ... this felt different, a lot different, and she didn't know how to process it or categorize it.

"Okay. Let's do it and see what happens."

Jack smiled. "Thank you ma'am." And then he got up to leave, putting the chair back perfectly in the corner. "Is there anything else I can get you before I go? I would stay longer, but I have paperwork to fill out and some more business to attend to."

Jack backed slowly toward the exit, smiling all the way. "No, I can ring for the nurse if I need anything."

He stopped for a moment. "Well, okay then. You have my cell if you need anything. I'll check on you again tonight to make sure everything's al right. Have a good day, Amanda."

And then he turned around once more and walked out of the hospital room. Amanda lay in her bed stunned, looking up at the white, painted ceiling. Her mind was a confused mixture of thoughts that seemed to collide into one another, like asteroids in space. She tried to sort them out, but couldn't. Nothing made sense up here, at least nothing made New York City sense. She understood the Big Apple, but ... Jackpine? She felt stupid just thinking and saying the name. *Jackpine?* Was it even a real place? It seemed foreign, like an alternate universe to her.

But he had asked her out, a man, a real man. He was undoubtedly the most attractive man she'd ever met, and she suddenly found herself wanting to follow this strange trail to find out where it ended. He seemed somehow ... pure to her. But that couldn't be ... she knew that. Men were not pure, and they had proven that to her over and over again. But ... and then she let her imagination run wild. What if Jack Ruger was different? What if he was special? The thought both intrigued and terrified her.

A wave of exhaustion suddenly overcame her, so Amanda closed her eyes. Within seconds she was fast asleep.

CHAPTER 7

Jackpine, Michigan

Sara Sinai liked the long, hard winters of the Keweenaw peninsula, with its gale-force winds, the sub-zero temperatures and the lack of sunlight for months on end. It took a special kind of person to live up here, in the isolation and harsh winter elements, but ... Sara had always prided herself in being different ... in being special. There had always been an interior toughness about her that no one could deny.

The average snowfall in Jackpine was 220 inches per year. Most of this snow was lake-effect and came compliments of Lake Superior, which is the largest freshwater lake by surface area and the third largest by volume of water on the entire planet. Sara liked the power of Lake Superior. Its deepest point was 1,333 feet, and Lake Superior was known to produce waves of up to 30 feet in height.

The Ojibwa Indians called the lake gichi-gami, but it was Henry Wadsworth Longfellow who simplified the name by calling it simply Gitche Gumee in his famous poem *The Song of Hiawatha*. French explorers of the 17th century had anglicized the name by calling it Superior. One of Sara's favorite songs was by Gordon Lightfoot and was titled *The Wreck of the Edmund Fitzgerald*. It was an ominous and scary tune that intrigued her, indeed, sent chills up and down her body every time she listened to it, which was often.

Despite Sara's love and respect for Lake Superior, she never ventured out onto the lake. She was prone to seasickness, and, quite frankly, the waves and sheer massiveness of the water terrified her. But that didn't stop her from loving the great inland lake.

She looked out the window now above her desk and saw the snow falling down. It was a lazy snow, one that came thick and heavy, but still, seemed to fall gently, softly, like the caress of a feather on her skin. Sara pulled the pink bathrobe closer against her body. She liked the warm softness of the fleece.

The computer screen in front of her remained blank, staring up at her, mocking her, daring her to type even one character that made sense and was worth keeping. But Sara couldn't do it. She was blocked and she knew it ... distracted by the terrible reality that she was being hunted and tracked like an animal. And the hunter was a woman named Amanda Walker from New York City.

Sara understood that most people would welcome a fat publishing contract with a big, New York City publisher, but ... Sara wasn't like the others. She valued her anonymity, her isolation, her ability to blend in with the other people of Jackpine, and, quite frankly, a multi-million-dollar book contract with a speaking tour and radio and TV interviews would certainly destroy all that. Her life, as she knew it, would suddenly and completely come to an end. Success came at a price, and that price was more than she wished to pay.

And then, of course, there was always her secret ... the one she guarded so closely that not even her best friends knew about it. And she would continue to guard it with her life. Nothing on this earth would ever convince or coerce her into relinquishing her lifestyle. Her isolation, her peace, her routine, all these things were her own private business ... her pearl of great price, and she would never give them up.

She looked back down at the blank screen, the cursor

flashing at her, steadily, obsessively, an unrelenting blinking orb that tormented her soul and threatened to drive her from sanity. Sara closed her blue eyes, purged her mind of Amanda Walker and all the concerns that were attached to her. She found her center, the deepest, richest part of herself, and ... she began to type, slaying the cursor, driving it back into the virtual depths of her computer.

Saturday, 4:30 - PM, Jackpine Police Department

"SO THE NAME SARA SINAI MEANS NOTHING TO YOU, sheriff?" Jack listened intently as the man on the other end of the line answered him. "I see. Well, I just thought I'd check. I had a person looking for her, and I offered to ask around."

There was a pause. "No, nothing nefarious I can assure you. I just know that you're acquainted with pretty much everyone in the county, and, if anyone knew her, it would be you."

And then Jack chuckled lightly. "Thanks Jeff. Let's hope it doesn't come to that. Thanks for your time."

Jack hung up the phone and swivelled his desk chair around to look out the window. The late-afternoon light was already fading away. That's one thing Jack didn't like about the upper peninsula weather. The winter days were just so darned short. It was harder to get things done, simply because people seemed to close up shop and head home earlier than normal.

He sighed and rose from his desk to put on his jacket. If he hurried, he'd have just enough time to talk to a few more people, then he could stop by Flo's place to get a bite to eat, before heading to the hospital. He left the office and locked the door behind him.

TWO HOURS LATER JACK WAS STANDING AT THE COUNTER of the diner talking to Florence. "I just need a burger and fries today, Flo. Something I can eat in the cruiser on my way to the hospital."

Florence smiled knowingly. "You want a Coke with that too?"

Jack didn't like the look she was giving him and he said so. "Why are you looking at me that way, Flo?"

She smiled broadly. "That girl sure is good lookin' ain't she."

Jack feigned ignorance. "It's just business, Flo. I promised her I'd try to help her find her friend. I'd do the same for anyone."

Florence popped her bubble gum. She always chewed Bubble Yum, the strawberry kind. "I spose so. Just business. It makes no never mind that she's drop-dead gorgeous and that she likes you."

Jack looked up suddenly and made eye contact with her. "So ... what makes you think she likes me? She's just here on business, you know. She'll be here for just a few days, then when she's done we'll never see her again."

Florence turned to the kitchen order window and placed the food ticket where it was quickly snatched up by her part-time cook. "I spose so. No use gettin' excited bout anything."

Jack shrugged his shoulders and then sat down at the counter to wait for his food. Flo leaned forward, with her elbows on the counter. "So, did ya find her friend yet? I been askin' all the diner folks about her and no one knows nothin'."

Jack smiled and shook his head. The diner was the center of social life here in Jackpine, and Florence was like the communication hub of the entire township. It was common knowledge that you never told Florence something that you didn't want the rest of the world to know. That wasn't to say that Flo couldn't keep a secret, because she could. You just had to specify which information was public and which was private.

"Nah, I come up cold. Even called the county sheriff, but nobody seems to know this woman exists."

Florence took the gum out of her mouth and twirled it around with her thumb and forefinger, before sticking it back inside. Jack hated to watch her do that.

"I spose if ya found this Sara girl, then Amanda would be mighty grateful." She smiled mischievously, but Jack ignored it and said nothing.

"Then again, the sooner ya find her, the sooner da city girl leaves da great white nort, eh?"

Jack smiled uncomfortably. "Careful, Flo. Your yooper accent is starting to slip out."

Florence Wentley had been raised in the upper peninsula, the yoo pee as people called it, and people born and raised north of the Mackinaw Bridge were commonly called yoopers. People south of the bridge were referred to as trolls. The yooper accent was primarily of Finnish, Scandinavian and French-Canadian origin, and that, mixed with the normal upper-midwest dialect, made for a language unique to northern Michigan, Wisconsin and Minnesota.

Jack was a native-born yooper, himself, but, he'd lost his accent while away at college and then later in the military. Jack had been away from Jackpine from age 18 to 28, and had only returned because the previous chief of police had been killed in the line of duty. It was a rare thing for police officers to die north of the bridge. And Fred Wentley (Flo's brother) had been Jack's foster parent after his real parents had died. After that, he'd grown to become a very close friend and mentor of Jack's.

"So, ya gonna ask her out?"

Jack smiled. "You're not jealous are you, Flo?"

She blushed. "Nope. I know my place, chief, and I'd rather be yer friend than yer unrequited lover."

Jack looked up at her, his face colored with surprise. "Unrequited? Where did you learn that word, Flo?"

Florence reached down and pulled a Kindle electronic reading device out from under the counter. It was already powered up and she showed Jack the screen. "I got dis Amazon prime account. I been readin' one a Sara Sinai's books on my kindle."

Jack made a surprised look by pursing his lips together. "So ... is she any good ... this Sara Sinai writer?"

Flo let her hand trail off the Kindle and down to her apron. "Don't rightly know yet. I guess so. I'm still a readin'."

Jack nodded. "Well, guess I'd better read it for myself then."

Florence laughed out loud. "Aw come on Jack, ya gotta be kiddin' me. Yer a man. Ya wouldn't get it at all."

Jack retaliated immediately. "Ah, don't sell me short, Flo. I'm a modern guy ... a real versatile man of the woods. I lived in the city for a while." He paused but then quickly added. "I've got depth, Flo."

Florence chuckled knowingly to herself and then went into the kitchen to check on his burger. Ten minutes later Jack walked out the door with a brown, paper bag full of food and a styrofoam cup of Coca-Cola.

On the drive to the hospital, Jack gobbled down his burger. It was a quarter pound of beef with lots of grease, just the way Jack liked it. He thought about Amanda Walker as he drove. There was an exotic attraction about her that belied his understanding. And he began to wonder to himself, *Why had he asked her out so quickly?* Jack hadn't dated since ... He let the memory slip on by him and back into the ages. Suffice it to say, the memory brought him pain, even now, and he had no wish to revisit it. And then he thought quietly to himself *Perhaps I should just let her go?*

And then his thoughts shifted to Florence. That woman knew too much and saw too much, subtle little things that most people didn't even notice. With her intuition and deductive reasoning powers, she could have been a great cop. Jack pulled his SUV cruiser into the hospital parking lot and parked.

CHAPTER 8

W HEN JACK WALKED INTO THE
hospital room, he heard Amanda talking on
the phone. She sounded nervous and agitat-
ed. Not wanting to intrude, Jack waited outside the door until
she was done.

"Yes, Mr. Harvath. I understand."

A nurse walked by Jack, and he politely smiled to her. She
kept going.

"I'm doing my best, sir. It's just that no one seems to know
who she is. It's like this woman doesn't even exist."

Jack tried not to listen, but ... for some reason he just wanted to eavesdrop.

"I'll do my best, sir."

"Yes, sir."

Jack knew he should walk away until she was done, but the
weaker part of him caused him to stay.

"I will report back to you every night sir, and if I find out
anything I'll call you before that."

"Yes, sir."

"I understand, sir."

"Yes, sir."

"Good bye, sir."

Jack waited several seconds before walking into her room.

When he finally came in she was pinching the bridge of her nose with her left thumb and forefinger and her head was down with her eyes closed. For a second he thought she was crying, but she wasn't.

When Amanda sensed someone in the room, she looked up and saw Jack standing there. Upon seeing the serious look on his face, she knew that he'd heard at least part of the conversation.

"How much of that did you hear?"

Jack looked down at the floor. "More than I should have, ma'am, and I apologize for that."

Despite being upset, Amanda looked much better than she had this morning. Jack waited for her to speak, but she said nothing.

"You ... look like you're feeling better tonight. Well ... at least physically, I mean."

Jack waited for her to answer, but she still said nothing. "Is there something wrong, Miss Walker?"

Amanda said nothing. Her eyes began to water and tears fell down her cheeks. She quickly moved her hand up to brush them away. She still hadn't answered him.

"Would you like me to leave? I can come back later if you like."

Amanda sniffed several times while Jack waited patiently at the door. Finally, Jack walked up to her bed and stood beside her. Part of him wanted to reach down and touch her. He knew that's what Florence would do. But ... another part of him, the man part, wanted to run out of the room and never come back. He took the middle of the road.

"Your boss sounds like a jerk."

Amanda laughed, even though she didn't want to. She found it difficult to laugh and cry at the same time.

"Oh, you're just being chivalrous. He's not such a bad guy, at least by New York standards." She hesitated. "People are different up here, Jack."

Jack Ruger reached over to the corner for the chair. It was

still there where he'd left it this morning. He sat down in it on the right side of the bed, closer this time.

"Things are different up here. I'll admit that. I think Jackpine and New York City must be polar opposites."

"Can I get one of those tissues please?"

Jack reached over to the food table, picked up the tissue box and handed it to her. Amanda took out two, brought them to her nose and blew. Jack turned away politely until she was finished.

"I realize that's not very ladylike, but ... I guess once you've given someone CPR a simple case of the sniffles isn't that big a deal."

Jack smiled. "I reckon not, ma'am."

Amanda turned to him and looked him squarely in the eyes. "Why do you talk like that?"

Jack raised his eyebrows just a tad. "Like what?"

"Oh, stop it, Jack. You know what I mean. You call me ma'am and Miss Walker and you always try to make me feel comfortable by asking what I need." She paused. "What's up with all that? What's your game?"

Jack sighed in his chair and then crossed one leg over the other before speaking. "So you're asking me why I'm so polite to you?"

"Well, kind of, but even New Yorkers are polite in their own, blunt and callus kind of way. But it's different with you. It's like you do it because you want to, and that confuses me."

Jack thought about that for a moment. He reached down to unzip his black, leather jacket before answering her. "It's just country manners, Amanda. I was raised that way and it comes out of me naturally. Don't you like it?"

Amanda fidgeted with the tissue box, tearing a corner of the cardboard. "It's not that I don't like it, Jack. It's that I can't bring myself to trust it."

He moved his right hand up to his chin and held it there for a moment as he thought about how much he should tell her. "I guess I understand that. I lived in New York City for four years. Well, north of there. People are different in the city. More interested in themselves, too busy to stop and help friends. They just mind their own business and try to stay out of each other's way."

Amanda tore off a corner of the tissue box and started ripping it into tiny pieces. "I can't believe you ever lived in New York."

"I graduated from West Point about 50 miles away, but I was able to visit the city enough to get to know it. I was on campus most of the time. It's a busy place, West Point."

Amanda looked at him in disbelief. "I just find it hard to believe that anyone from here could ever function in a more intricate culture like New York City or in the military." She looked out the window at the snow. "You just seem so ... relaxed here, so happy, so ... at home."

Jack smiled for the first time during their conversation. "I am happy here, but I was happy in the army as well. As a general rule I don't remain in unhappy situations for very long. Life is too short for that."

"What did you do in the military?"

"I started out in the infantry, but then ended up as an MP. That happens a lot in the army. Mother army tends to send you where you're needed instead of where you want to go."

Just then the nurse came in to take her vitals. Everything was normal, and she was soon out of the room.

"Did you have to go to the fighting over in Iraq?"

Jack shook his head. "No, I was in Afghanistan. Just for one tour."

She waited for him to tell her more, but apparently that's all she was going to get out of him on that subject. She'd heard that people who fight in wars don't like to talk about it, so she didn't press him on it. He quickly changed the subject.

"So, how are you feeling today?"

Amanda tried to smile. "Much better. I'm starting to get bored here. The doctor says I can be released tomorrow morning, provided everything still looks good."

Jack glanced over on her tray table and saw the Sara Sinai romance book titled *Forever Love* and nodded his head at it.

"I see you're reading Sara Sinai too?"

Amanda reached over to the tray and picked it up. It was about 175 pages long in five by eight inch format.

"Yeah, it's pretty good. I was surprised by it." And then she hesitated as if choosing her words carefully. "It's not like the rest of the genre."

Jack looked interested.

"How so?"

"Well, to begin with, there's no sex in it. That's very unusual for romance novels. Sara's books are clean, but ... I don't know, they still seem interesting some how. I feel like she's speaking to me directly, just like you and I are talking right now. It's really weird and I can't explain it."

"So you like it then?"

Amanda thought for moment. "Yeah, I guess I do. Even though I don't understand why. After reading her book, it's strange, but I felt clean, like I've just gotten done taking a bubble bath. If that makes any sense at all."

Jack shook his head from side to side. "Nope. I've never taken a bubble bath, so that means nothing to me. But I do take showers from time to time."

Amanda laughed and this time her head didn't hurt. She turned the paperback book over in her hand and looked at the back cover.

"I wonder who did the cover design for her. It's very unorthodox, not like other romance novels at all."

Jack slipped his jacket off and tossed it on the floor close to the wall. "Well, perhaps you could ask her just as soon as you find her."

Amanda's face clouded over. "But what if I can't find her?" And then she made eye contact with him. "Did you get a chance to look for her today?"

Jack sighed and looked down at the floor before answering. "Well, I spent quite a bit of time on the phone asking around and Flo talked to everyone at the diner, but ... no one knows anything about her." He shrugged. "I don't think she's here, Amanda."

"Can't you like put out an ABP on her or something? I've got to find her!"

Jack laughed out loud and then corrected her. "I think you mean APB. That stands for All Points Bulletin, and we can't do that unless we have reasonable suspicion that a crime has been or is about to be committed."

Amanda set the book back down on the food tray. Then she crossed her arms and seemed to pout. Jack seemed amused by her response.

"So, what are you going to do if you don't find her?"

She looked down at the tiny pile of cardboard bits that she'd torn up on her bedsheet and sighed. "Well, I guess I'll polish up my resume and start looking for another job."

A troubled look came over Jack's face. He looked down at his black, high-top leather boots. They were polished to a high sheen, with little drops of speckled water on them from the melted snow.

"I find it hard to believe that your boss would fire you for one tiny failure. Why would he do that? It doesn't seem reasonable to me."

The look on her face changed slightly, as if she was no longer in the room with him and looking at something very far away. "He probably wouldn't fire me, at least not right away, but ... "

Jack finished the thought for her. "You're afraid it will affect your future there with the company, things like raises and promotions and things like that?"

Amanda nodded slowly. Jack felt bad for her, and a part of him wanted to tell her the truth, but ... he just couldn't bring himself to do it. Too much was at stake. So, he let the opportunity pass him by.

"Well, Miss Walker, I will keep looking for her, and if I find anything out I'll certainly let you know."

Amanda sensed a change in Jack's demeanor. He kept going back and forth from formal to informal and then back again to formal. First he called her Amanda, then ma'am, then Miss Walker again. If his mood swings got any worse she'd suffer from whiplash. Jack seemed more complex than any man she'd ever known.

"Thank you, Jack."

Neither of them talked again. It was as if someone had thrown a breaker switch and the power to the conversation was turned off. After a few more seconds of silence, Jack got up and retrieved his jacket from the floor. This was not satisfying, and Amanda didn't like it.

"Well, I'm glad you're feeling better, ma'am. I'll be back around noon tomorrow to take you where you need to go. Please let me know if you need anything before then."

Suddenly, Amanda felt angry. Was he toying with her? Why, just this morning he'd asked her out to dinner, and now ... it was like they were business associates.

"Now Chief Ruger, I can't let you go out of your way like that. It would be an imposition."

But Jack waved her off. "No, no, now I insist. It's the least we can do. After all, you're a visitor and we need to show you hospitality."

Amanda wanted to jump off the bed and slap him, but she didn't have the strength ... yet. The prideful, New Yorker in her wanted to lash out at him, to yell and scream, but ... she knew that would be irrational. Besides, she needed him to give her a ride back to her car in Jackpine. *Jackpine* ... what a stupid name for a city!

"Why thank you, Chief Ruger. I appreciate it very much."

Jack was done putting his jacket on, and he backed toward the door, his eyes lingering on her every move. Amanda couldn't help but wonder *why is he looking at me that way?* But it no longer mattered. Whatever attraction she'd felt for him before, was totally erased.

"Good night, ma'am." And then he was gone.

Amanda lie on the bed, feeling used and abused and suddenly, so very alone. She hated Jackpine and everyone in it. After all, they didn't even have Wi-Fi.

Amanda turned to look out the window of her room. She watched Jack get into his blue SUV and drive away, his headlights fading into the night.

CHAPTER 9

THE **MARQUETTE BRANCH PRISON** was built in 1889 and contained both Level 1 and Level 5 inmates. Level 1 inmates are deemed to require less supervision, as they have a tendency to obey the rules and to get along socially with the other inmates. They aren't, as a general rule, incredibly violent; they just want to do their time, get out, and either start a new life, or to continue on with their interrupted life of crime.

Level 5 inmates aren't like that. Most of them are extremely violent and pose a high risk of escape as they have long sentences and don't have all that much to lose. Level 5 inmates murder for fun, and the rapists hurt their victims more for control than sex, or, in some cases, to satisfy some other complicated desire that they themselves don't understand.

Inmate number 56231 was Level 5. The perimeter of the Level 5 complex is protected by a concrete wall, by concertina wire (think metal wire surrounded with razor blades) a sophisticated electronic detection system, as well as eight gun towers. Because of all this, it was highly unlikely that any prison breaks would be successful from Level 5. So inmate 56231 simply bribed an administrative worker to go into the computer and have himself transferred into the Level 1 facility. He then escaped the very same hour before anyone noticed the mistake. It was genius, really, but had cost him over 20,000 dollars up front. But then again, it was a small price for freedom, and the money he'd spent didn't belong to him anyway.

Now he waited on the edge of the park to rendezvous with that same prison worker to pay him the agreed-upon balance of 50,000 dollars. Why the worker believed that a sociopathic killer would keep his word once out of prison was a mystery to 56231, but, if the plan worked, it wouldn't matter.

He saw the headlights of the car round the corner and watched as it parked beside the evergreen tree. It was a newer four-wheel-drive pick-up truck with a cap, and would serve his purposes perfectly. Inmate 56231 watched the man get out of the vehicle and stand beside it. He waited five minutes just to make sure the jail worker was alone. Then he raised the 22 caliber rifle to his shoulder and took aim, carefully placing the crosshairs in the center of the man's ocular cavity. He pressed the trigger lightly, and the 40 grain, lead, round-nose bullet streaked toward its target traveling 1,200 feet per second.

The sound of the rifle shot was minimal and soon echoed out and was lost in the howling of the wind. The shot was perfect, and the man went down in an untidy heap. After that, it was simply a matter of dragging the body into the nearest snow bank and burying it beneath three feet of cold, white snow. He'd already listened to the weather forecast, and over a foot of snow would erase all signs of foul play by morning. And by then he would be long gone.

Inmate 56231 brushed the snow away from his clothing before getting into the truck. It was still running and was very warm inside. A quick search revealed 17,000 dollars cash in the glove box and a nine millimeter Glock Model 19 in the console. The inmate laughed out loud. His escape had cost him only 3,000 dollars of someone else's hard-earned money.

First order of business was to kill his bank-heist partner who was waiting for him just outside Newberry so they could meet up and recover the rest of the money from the bank robbery. Inmate 56231 didn't like loose ends, but he had to be careful, as his former partner might be feeling the same way about him. After that, he'd drive back west to Jackpine and deal with some unfinished business. Once that was done ... perhaps Canada for a while.

He put the truck in reverse, backed out and then pulled away from the crime scene eager to get something to eat. His mouth began to water. He hadn't had a Burger King Whopper combo meal in over four years. Tonight he would splurge ... and super-size it.

Sunday, 7AM - Baraga County Memorial Hospital

"So why is Jack mad at me all of a sudden?"

Florence glanced away from the road just long enough to make brief eye contact with Amanda. "For land's sakes, girl. What makes ya think Jack is mad at ya?"

Amanda looked out the window as they pulled out of the hospital parking lot. "Well ... I don't know. He was supposed to pick me up this morning is all. And ... well, he was acting kind of strange last night."

This got Flo's attention. "Strange? How's that?"

Amanda thought about it for a moment. She didn't quite understand it herself, so she just blurted it out. "Well, yesterday morning we had a real good talk, and he even asked me out to dinner ..."

Florence interrupted her. "Jack asked ya out to dinner?"

Amanda nodded. "Yes, he was going to take me to the city and buy me dinner."

The other woman furled her brow just a bit. "Really."

But then she said nothing more. The silence was uncomfortable for Amanda, but Florence seemed quite content with it. Finally, Amanda broke the silence.

"So ... what do you think?"

"'Bout what?"

The younger girl let out an impatient sigh, then she ran the fingers of her left hand through her honey-blonde hair before answering. "What do you think about Jack asking me out, and then not showing up to give me a ride back to Jackpine?"

Florence chuckled softly to herself. "Land's sakes, girl. He's a man so don't be 'spectin' him to make much sense."

She was quiet a moment before continuing. "He stopped by the diner 'n told me he had some cop business ta do, and asked if I'd pick ya up? That don't sound so weird ta me."

Amanda looked down at her lap and fidgeted with the seat belt. "It's just that ... you know ... I thought he ..." But she let the words trail off into nothingness. Florence finished the thought for her.

"Ya thought Jack was hot ta trot on ya?"

Amanda blushed and was taken slightly aback by Flo's bluntness. "Well ... I wouldn't exactly put it that way, but ... you know ... I thought he might be interested."

Florence nodded her head. "Well, of course he's interested in ya. I mean fer god's sake, girl! Look at ya! Yer young 'n gorgeous, 'n skinny, 'n ya still got all yer teeth. Jack 'd be crazy not ta look at ya twice."

Amanda's face took on a glazed-over and confused stare. "Florence, has anyone ever told you that you have a funny way of putting things?"

Florence put on her turn signal and made a left onto the two-lane highway. "Nope. Can't say they have." She finished the turn as she straightened the steering wheel back out.

"But ya gotta understand, girl, that yer in Jackpine now. I reckon yer gonna hear 'n see stuff ya ain't seen before.

Amanda nodded. "I know. I've figured that out. Jackpine is nothing like New York City, and I know I'm the stranger here. But I just can't help but think that we were connecting, that he wanted to take our relationship to the next level?"

Florence started laughing out loud ... so loud that she had to pull over to the side of the road. She turned on her emergency flashers and turned to look Amanda in the eyes.

"Amanda, ya gotta be the silliest girl in 'da yoo-pee. I mean I never heard nothin' so silly in my life."

Amanda was shocked and didn't know what to say, but it didn't matter because Florence just kept right on talking.

"Ya ain't got no relationship with Jack. Ya hardly know the guy, 'n he hardly knows you!"

Amanda felt very uncomfortable now, and she wished she'd never broached the topic. She didn't know what to say, so she said nothing. But Florence wasn't about to shut up.

"Let me tell ya 'bout Jack, honey. He was born 'n raised here in Jackpine. His parents were murdered when he was ten years old. After that my brother, Fred, 'n his wife took 'm in and raised him up. Fred was the Chief of Police fer Jackpine his whole life. When Jack was 18 he went to West Point. Then ta the army 'n on ta Afghanistan where he got shot. But he healed up good, but then my brother and his wife got shot 'n killed by some guy just passin' through."

She stopped for a few seconds, then looked over the snow-covered field to her left. There was a funeral home in the lot, and Florence noted how convenient it was to have it so close to the hospital. Then she went on.

"Jack felt guilty fer leavin' ... felt like it was his fault that Fred 'n Irma got killed, cuz he weren't there ta help 'em. So's he quit the army and came back here ta Jackpine 'n took over as the chief. Jack fell in love with Carrie Parker 'n they was fixin' ta get married, but then she came down with cancer 'n she died."

Flo's voice wavered just a bit, and then she looked back through the windshield, and Amanda couldn't see her eyes anymore. There was silence for several seconds, but then Florence rallied her spirits and pressed on.

"That's done been over a year now, 'n Jack's been on the mend. He got quiet on us 'n we worry 'bout him sometimes." And then Florence grew silent again. Finally, when Amanda didn't respond, Florence kept talking.

"I love Jack Ruger, like he was my son, my brother 'n my

lover all rolled up in one guy. So's if ya got any ideas on hurtin' 'em, then ya better think again, sweetie. Cuz all of us here in Jackpine love the man, 'n we wouldn't take kindly ta ya hurtin' 'em." She paused. Amanda's eyes had started to well up upon hearing Jack's life story, but she wasn't yet ready to respond.

Florence reached over with her right hand and placed it on Amanda's shoulder. "I like ya, girl. But ya gotta understand the rules 'round here. Jack is family, 'n nobody messes with family in Jackpine. Ya got it?"

Amanda nodded her head up and down, but didn't say anything. She had the feeling like she'd just been drinking straight emotions from a high-pressure fire hose, and she felt overwhelmed.

And that's when Amanda began to realize just how selfish and narcissistic she'd been. She'd been looking at Jack through her own egocentric prism, analyzing his actions through her own wants and needs, drawing conclusions about him based solely on her own feelings with no regard for his life and his pain.

First he'd lost his parents, then his foster parents, then his fiance. Then he'd given up his career out of a sense of responsibility to protect and defend his home town. No wonder they loved him so much. Amanda wondered what it would be like to be loved that much. But she hadn't a clue. All she cared about was her career, her salary and her apartment in New York.

Suddenly, Amanda felt hollow, like all the meaning and purpose had been sucked out of her. She turned to the right of the car and looked at the funeral home. So much of Jack's life had been equated with death. Death and loss. She felt sad for him.

Florence squeezed Amanda's shoulder lightly. Amanda turned her head toward her, tears finally running unabated down her cheeks. "It's okay, Flo. I won't hurt him."

And with that girl-to-girl understanding, the two women

hugged in the car. They both cried for a few minutes, then Florence turned off the emergency flashers and pulled back out onto the two-lane road. They left the hospital quickly behind them. The whole drive back to Jackpine, Amanda couldn't help but wonder how one short conversation, one event, one simple hug, could alter her life so profoundly and eternally. And, at that point in time, on that two-lane country highway, Amanda Walker started to change. She began thinking about others before herself.

CHAPTER 10

JACK SAT AT HIS DESK, STARING VA-cantly out the window into the cold, frozen air of the upper peninsula. That one phone call had changed everything. His home phone had rung at 5AM this morning, which was highly unusual. And then when he'd heard the warden's voice, his heart had sunk down into his bowels. There had been an escape, and he was giving Jack a courtesy call that turned out to be an ominous warning. Inmate number 56231 had busted out. Jack looked down at the paper file on his desk.

There was a black and white prison photo of the escapee, whose real name was Robert Lee Harper. Robert Harper, or, Bobbie Lee as most people called him, had gone on a killing spree several years back while Jack had still been in the army. The spree had started in Tennessee and ended in Jackpine, where his best friend and mentor, his foster father, Fred Wentley, had been shot in the back and killed, but not before Fred had returned fire and wounded the man. Fred's wife had also been killed in the crossfire, making it an extra traumatic moment for Jack, now having lost two sets of parents to early death.

Jack had taken leave from the military, to attend the funeral. After coming home to Jackpine, his sense of duty and obligation for the town and his friends had overwhelmed him. He'd eventually resigned his commission and taken up the trail of Bobbie Lee. It had taken two months, but Jack finally tracked Bobbie Lee down in western Montana. Bobbie Lee hadn't come peacefully, and that was fine by Jack. The ensuing gunfight had left Bobbie Lee severely wounded but alive. After the trial, he'd been sentenced to life in prison with no chance of parole in Michigan. For the past eight years he'd been serving time in Marquette Branch Prison as a Level 5 inmate.

But now he was out again, and Jack knew in his heart that he would be coming back for his revenge as Bobbie Lee had promised at the closing of the trial.

Jack picked up the photo and looked at it again. His eyes focused, burning the image into his mind. Then he tossed it back onto his desk and leaned back into his chair. It squeaked as he did so. It always squeaked, but Jack was so focused that he couldn't hear it now.

And then he thought about Amanda Walker. She was indeed beautiful, and young, and intelligent. He hadn't seen a woman that beautiful since ... He let the thought slip away, and reached down to his desk drawer on the right of him. He opened it up and took out the picture frame. He still missed Carrie, more than ever. She'd had a beautiful heart and soul, but ... now she was gone. He took one last look at her and then put the frame back into the desk drawer. He closed it up and wouldn't look at it again until this was all over. And he wouldn't think about Amanda Walker either. There was no time for it. He had to focus. And, most importantly ... watch his back. His life depended on it.

8AM Sunday - Newberry, Michigan - 170 Miles East of Jackpine

BOBBIE LEE PULLED OFF FALLS ROAD NORTH OF Newberry and south of Fourmile Corner. It was just a little logging trail, but he knew no one would be interested in what he was doing up there. It was pretty remote, and the owners of the property were non-residents, probably trolls from down Detroit way. He was thankful for the four-wheel-drive truck with high clearance as he got up some speed to power through the snow blocking his way. When he got about a quarter mile off the main road, he did a three-point turn so that he was facing the main road again, just in case he needed a quick getaway.

He pulled out his newly acquired cell phone and fired up the GPS. Then he put on his arctic Carhartts, hat and fleece-lined mittens. After that he put the light-duty snow camo over the Carhartts. It was going to be a long, hard hike, but he knew it was necessary to achieve surprise. His former business partner would undoubtedly anticipate that Bobbie Lee would try to kill him, so he would appropriately try to kill Bobbie Lee first. It was nothing personal ... just good, smart business practice. Never leave any loose ends. Never trust the people you work with, especially when money is involved. And there was close to a million dollars at stake on this occasion. Bobbie Lee had kept the location of the money a secret from his partner after being imprisoned. Even when Ronnie Talsma had come to visit him personally at the prison, Bobbie Lee had refused to give up the location. He had, however, given him the secondary location of a lesser amount of money, with the promise of much more if he would help arrange his prison break. It was Ronnie who had set up the escape with the administrative aid at Marquette prison. But Bobbie Lee wasn't naive enough to think it was out of anything less than good, old-fashioned, selfish greed. He was well aware, that if he wasn't careful, he could end up dead on this one.

He pulled the knapsack out of the back of the extended cab and put it on his back. Then he took out the rifle case and laid it on the tailgate before opening it up. Inside was a rifle he considered adequate for the job: a Smith & Wesson Model 10 M&P, long-series hunting rifle. It was chambered in 308 Winchester and extremely accurate within 1,000 yards, assuming the shooter was proficient, and Bobbie Lee, growing up hunting in Tennessee, was very good out to that range.

He fixed the sling to the right length and then double-checked the 10-round magazine before ramming it into the mag well and pulling back on the charging handle. He double-checked to make sure the safety selector was on, then he set the rifle back on the tailgate. Next, he donned his drop-leg holster so it rode on his right thigh and chambered a round in his Glock Model 19 pistol. He liked Glock because of their reliability; this was important to him, because Bobbie Lee had a tendency to abuse his toys. He selected two extra 15-round mags and fastened them in the pockets of his holster. He already had an extra fully-loaded 10-round mag for the 308 in one of the pockets of the knapsack, just in case things went south.

Bobbie Lee attached his snow shoes to his hiking boots and then stood up to give his gear one final check. He slung the rifle onto his shoulder, put up the tailgate and then locked the truck up. Bobbie Lee was age 35 and getting much too old for this.

He took one last look at the truck and then picked up his GPS. He input the grid coordinates and set off across the woods for the rendezvous point. If he hurried, he could get there several hours ahead of Ronnie.

Sunday, 10AM - Jackpine Diner, Late Afternoon

AMANDA HAD RECOVERED HER RENTAL CAR, AND WAS now seated at the counter of the Jackpine Diner. She looked around the room at the empty tables, wondering how Florence managed to stay in business. She'd been here for almost two hours and not a single person had entered the establishment.

Suddenly, the bell over the door came to life, startling Amanda so much she flinched. She turned just in time to see an old man in his eighties walk slowly through the door.

Florence, who was in the back, heard the bell and came out to the dining area.

"Hey, Tom. How's it goin' eh!"

Tom Leonard leaned heavily on his cane and looked up briefly on his trek to the counter. Amanda stared at him as he walked, wondering how he would make it up to the bar stool. The old man didn't answer right away. He just slowly hobbled up and jumped lightly onto the stool with an audible groan.

"Hey, Flo. I'm still alive, and that's nine tenths of the battle. How come yer not at service this mornin'?"

Florence smiled. She always asked him the same question at this time every day, and he always gave her the same answer.

"Somethin' come up. I'll go twice next Sunday. Ya here fer yer pasty?"

"You betcha, Flo. I think it's the only thing keepin' me alive these days. Heavy on the lard will ya?"

Florence smiled. "So you want chicken again?"

The old man placed both hands up on the counter top and leaned down hard.

"Not today, Flo. I got my fill a chickens these days. Give me the venison."

Florence shook her head from side to side. "Now, Tom, ya know dern well that I can't sell wild game here. It's against state law."

Tom laughed. "Yup. I know it. But it's the deer meat I got a hankerin' for, so hop to and cook it up for me, before I lose my temper an start a whippin' on ya!"

Florence tried to look stern, but failed. "Tell ya what I'll do, Tom. I'll give ya the beef that tastes an awful lot like venison. Will that suit ya?"

Tom looked over at Amanda and then back to Florence. "I don't care. Just do somethin' fore I die a old age here."

Florence smiled just a tad and then disappeared into the kitchen to start cooking. The old man looked over at Amanda again and barked at her harshly.

"What ya lookin' at woman! Ain't ya ever seen a old man afore?"

Amanda started to talk, but he cut her off. "Who are ya anyways? I ain't never seen ya afore."

Amanda tried to answer, but the bell over the door rang again as Jack Ruger walked into the diner. He strode confidently up to the counter and stood beside Tom Leonard.

"Hey, Tom. How's it going?"

"Ah, hey Jack. I been runnin' around busy as a one-legged man in a butt-kickin' contest."

Jack ignored the comment, like it was as natural as the sunrise. "So, Tom. Did you apologize to Henry and replace those chickens yet?"

Tom pursed his lips together tightly and frowned. "I done told ya I would. I called him up, but no body answered. I'll try again tomorrow."

Jack frowned as well, but his eyes kept their twinkle. "You call him back today, Tom. I don't want this to fester till morning. Just get it done. I want your word on that."

Tom hesitated and Jack moved a little closer and whispered something in his ear that Amanda couldn't quite make out.

"Okay, fine! I'll git it done tonight! You are such a pain in the butt!"

And then Tom looked over at Amanda and then back at Jack. "But ya gotta tell this youngster here ta stop hittin' on me. It makes me feel cheap 'n dirty!"

Jack tried not to laugh but couldn't hold it in. He smiled at Amanda with his blue eyes and she melted inside.

"Is that right, Ma'am. Have you been harassing this young man?"

Amanda's first response was to be angry, but ... she thought better of it and surprised Jack with her response.

"Ya dern right I been a hittin'on 'em. This here gorgeous hunk a man flesh. Why any woman would be proud to take him home for the night."

Her voice sounded ridiculous as she tried unsuccessfully

to impersonate a country accent. Jack laughed out loud with no attempt to hide it. He winked at Amanda and then stepped around the counter. "Is Flo in the back?"

Amanda nodded as Jack walked by and disappeared into the kitchen. She glanced over at Tom and smiled slyly.

"Careful lady. My spirit is willin' but the flesh is weak. I got a bad heart ta boot."

Amanda hopped up off the stool and started to follow Jack into the kitchen. "Don't be such a tease, Tom."

The old man clutched at his chest and smiled softly. "Be still my beatin' heart."

THIS WAS AMANDA'S FIRST TIME IN FLO'S KITCHEN, BUT it was much like any other small restaurant, with a large gas range and stainless steel sinks and storage cabinets. She saw Florence and Jack over by the gas range, talking in hushed tones. Florence held a sheet of paper in her left hand. It had writing and a photo on it, but Amanda couldn't make out the details. Jack glanced over and stopped talking.

Amanda looked at them curiously before speaking. They were obviously hiding something from her. "What's going on, Jack?"

Jack didn't answer her. He started to move toward the door, but Florence reached out and grabbed his arm. "You should tell her, Jack." He hesitated, looked at Amanda and then back at Florence. Finally, he resigned himself.

"Fine." He looked back at Amanda. "You need to leave Jackpine as soon as you can. Right this moment would be best. You should probably get back to New York City. That would be safer for you."

Amanda looked at Florence for verification, but Flo said nothing. Jack handed her a sheet of paper like the one Florence had, and she looked down and read it. Then she looked back up at Jack. "What does this have to do with me having to leave?"

Jack turned away, letting Flo's hand fall to her side. "You

tell her, Flo. I got work to do." And then he left the kitchen. Amanda heard the bell over the door as he walked out into the cold, blowing snow.

Florence looked down at the paper in her hand, then back up at Amanda. "This is the guy who killed my brother, Fred 'n my sister'n-law Irma. He just broke out of prison. He'll be headin' this way."

Amanda thought for a moment. "Why would he come here? Seems to me he'd try to get as far away from here as possible."

Florence shook her head from side to side, and then reached over to pull Amanda closer to her. While she made Tom's pasty, she told Amanda the whole story. When she was done, Amanda understood the danger. But still ... a part of her didn't want to leave Jackpine.

CHAPTER 11

<u>*Sunday, 10AM, Newberry, Michigan*</u>

BOBBIE LEE LAY ON A THICK BED OF pine needles beneath the overhanging boughs of a small white pine, watching the secluded parking area about 200 yards away. So far no one had come, but he was still early. He had scooped up as many pine needles as possible and used them as an insulating cushion to place his neoprene pad on top of. He knew that he'd have to lay perfectly still for his plan to work, because if they saw him, then he'd be the one in mortal danger instead of the other way around.

His rifle was already in position, locked and loaded, ready to deliver its lethal payload, and Bobbie Lee was psychologically ready to press the trigger, even eager to do so. The fore end of the rifle was resting atop his pack to keep it out of the snow, and to give it a solid support for the final shot. Two-hundred yards was an easy shot with this rifle, but he was leaving nothing to chance. Even easy shots could be missed if you didn't follow the principles of good marksmanship.

Bobbie Lee opened up several cellophane packs of body warmers and placed the adhesive backing on the neoprene pad. It was better to be too warm than too cold, because he may have to wait here on the ground for several hours. He'd stolen most of the equipment, including the rifle and ammo from a small mom and pop gun store east of Marquette. He liked to rob the smaller stores, which usually operated out of a garage or pole barn, simply because the security was usually less sophisticated. As soon as his schedule slowed down, he'd take the time to have professional grade identification made, and then he could buy anything he wanted, but for now he'd have to steal what he needed or pay cash.

He waited for an hour in the cold, and then he heard the far-away sound of a car engine. Bobbie Lee listened carefully as it drew closer. Then he heard the sound of another. Five minutes later both vehicles were parked 200 yards away in the clearing below him. The presence of two vehicles instead of one confirmed his notion that Ronnie Talsma was going to kill him. But, of course, he didn't hold that against the man since he was about to kill Ronnie first.

Bobbie Lee thought carefully about the most efficient and risk-free way to handle this scenario. If he shot one man right away, the survivor would duck down behind cover, making it very difficult to kill the second man. He decided to wait for a better opportunity, one with a higher chance of success. The last thing he wanted was to have to close the distance and risk a close-range shoot out.

He could hear their voices now, but couldn't make out what they were saying. Then Ronnie pointed to a pine tree about fifty yards further to the east. The other man nodded and went to his SUV. He pulled out snow camo and a gun case. Bobbie watched patiently as the man readied himself and his gear. He looked like he'd done this before. He was a professional, and Ronnie must have paid him quite a sum.

Bobbie Lee moved his monocular back to Ronnie, who was looking around nervously. This made Bobbie Lee smile. He moved the monocular back over to the man who was to assassinate him and chuckled. The man was ready now and talked briefly to Ronnie, who quickly looked at his watch and pointed again to the pine tree. The man walked through the snow and climbed the tree.

As the man climbed, Bobbie Lee made mental preparations. He started to breathe more slowly, to slow his heart-rate and to calm himself as much as possible. About thirty seconds later he took one last look at the man climbing the tree. He was about twenty feet off the ground. Bobbie Lee put the butt of his rifle to his right shoulder and eased his eye down to the scope. He decided to shoot Ronnie first, just to make sure he didn't get away.

The cross-hairs moved down onto the center of Ronnie's body, and then up just a hair. At this angle the bullet should rip right through the heart and into the spine. He took a deep breath, and then slowly relaxed, letting out the air as he pressed back to take the slack out of the trigger. He hit a slight wall on the trigger, then pressed through it.

The recoil and noise surprised him as it sometimes did on a good shot. Ronnie collapsed immediately, confirming the spine shot. Bobbie Lee quickly re-situated his body as he moved the position of the rifle to get a good shot at the man who now perched on a pine branch, frozen near the top of the tree. The white snow camo he was wearing, outlined his torso against the backdrop of green pine boughs. It had been a bad clothing selection, allowing Bobbie Lee to line up the cross-hairs perfectly. The rifle barked again. He watched through the scope as the man tried desperately to hang onto the branch with his gloved hands. Five seconds later he fell, hitting several branches on the way to the ground. Bobbie Lee reasoned to himself, *if the bullet hadn't killed him, then the fall certainly had.*

He moved the scope down to the front of the vehicle, where Ronnie lay in an ever-widening pool of his own blood. Bobbie Lee lay still for five more minutes, every minute or so looking through the scope to check for movement. They were both dead. It was obvious to him now.

Carefully, he moved to his knees, and moved the selector switch to safe. Then he gathered up his pack, carefully stowed all his gear back inside, and then hunted for the two empty brass casings. He found them and shoved them into the pocket of his Carhartts. He smoothed out the pine needles again as well as the snow around him before putting his snowshoes back on his boots. After the snow tonight, all evidence of his presence would be erased forever. *Or so he thought.*

One last time, he moved the monocular up to his right eye and scanned the area. He looked down at the dead bodies again just to make sure. As far as Bobbie Lee was concerned, this phase of the operation was over. He put the monocular back into his breast pocket and slung his rifle over his right shoulder before walking into the forest back to his truck.

Now, just one more order of business ... and he couldn't stop thinking about Jack Ruger. He had something special planned for him ... something very special.

Sunday, Noon - Jackpine Police Headquarters

JACK RUGER SAT BEHIND HIS DESK, CONTEMPLATING HIS next move. Bobbie Lee Harper was out there, stalking him, watching him, could, indeed even be looking at him at this very moment. He knew that Harper was an excellent shot out to 1,000 yards, but Jack didn't believe he would die by a sniper's bullet. No ... Bobby Lee would make it personal. He would exact vengeance up close in the most intimate and painful way possible.

Most men would be afraid. Most men would run. But Jack Ruger was not most men. And there was something that Bobbie Lee didn't know. Jack Ruger wanted him to come for him. He wanted Bobbie Lee to try and kill him. Ever since their last shoot-out, when Jack had wounded and captured Bobbie Lee, Jack had wanted a rematch, had indeed been yearning and begging for another opportunity to avenge the death of his friend and mentor, Fred Wentley.

And that vengeful feeling didn't sit too well with Jack's badge.

Of course, Bobbie Lee deserved to die, and the death of

him would make society better and safer, but ... to want to kill a man ... well, that was a new emotion for Jack. He'd become a cop, not for revenge, but for the honor of protecting and defending the people of Jackpine. He'd always possessed a strong protective instinct, and, perhaps that was why he'd also joined the military in the first place. Jack was a full-fledged and natural-born warrior, and to pretend to be something different would be impossible for him.

Jack's mind drifted back to the first time he'd met Bobbie Lee Harper. It had been in Escanaba over a hundred miles southeast of Jackpine. It wasn't often you met a man because you were hunting him down to kill him, but, that had been the case with Jack and Bobbie Lee. Their's was an unusual relationship, one born of fire and blood and death. And there was only one way it could end: one of them had to die.

Jack still felt conflicted about their gun fight. Jack had missed the man's heart by less than an inch, thereby, unwittingly sparing the man's life. He should have followed up with a second shot, but ... Jack would not make that mistake again.

Jack reached down with his right hand and unholstered his pistol. It wasn't the kind of handgun that most law enforcement officers carried. It was designed for precision ... deadly precision. He brought the gun up and placed it on his desk. It was a Walther Q5 Match pistol. It had a five-inch barrel and the blue trigger had been smoothed out special and was very light on the press, making him deadly accurate out to greater distances. Jack had mounted a Dual illuminated Trijicon RMR red dot sight, which served to enhance his precision even more. This was a gun designed originally for competition shooting, but Jack had modified it for one thing and one thing only ... to kill bad guys. When he finally met Bobbie Lee again ... he would not miss.

And then he thought about Amanda Walker. He cared about her, but she had to leave town and leave town now. Her absence would solve a lot of problems for him. First, he'd be able to focus on hunting down Bobbie Lee, thereby enhancing his own chances of survival. Second, it would stave off the emotional conflict he was feeling about being attracted to her. He felt guilt, overwhelming guilt at trying to move on after Carrie's death. He loved her so much that a part of him wanted to grieve forever, to never look at another woman. But another part of him ... the hidden and secret part of him that was lonely, wanted to scoop Amanda into his arms and press her close. She was a beautiful woman, and it had been such a long time since he'd held a beautiful woman in his arms.

He thought about Carrie a moment longer. He resisted the urge to open the desk drawer and look at her picture again, like he'd already done five times today. No, he needed to focus. He needed to put both Carrie and Amanda, both the old and the new totally out of his mind. Because he knew, in his heart of hearts, that if he didn't, if he lost focus ... then Bobbie Lee would kill him for sure.

Sunday, 1PM - Munising, Michigan

THE DOGPATCH RESTAURANT HAD BEEN IN MUNISING for as long as Bobbie Lee could remember, and he was thankful to see that it was still open. He pulled into the parking lot in the back, as far away from the buildings as he could get to avoid surveillance cameras, and took a quick look around. He glanced over at the entrance and saw the lil' Abner mural on the wall and smiled. Bobbie Lee knew that Daisy Mae was just a cartoon character, but ... he turned away and scanned the surrounding area. Seeing no police cars, he got out, locked the doors and walked toward the entrance, all the while looking around the parking lot. Parking areas were dangerous and there was no telling what kind of scum might be hiding out, ready to ambush and rob him. He glanced at the mural to his left as he approached the door and spoke out loud as if Daisy Mae were real. "Yer lookin' sweet today, Daisy."

Bobbie Lee opened the door and stepped inside. He took one look around before entering further. He noticed a few locals, but no cops or anyone else that got his attention. He quickly walked to a back corner and sat with his back to the wall. He could still see the entrance from here and he was out of the line of sight for most people.

The waitress saw him and walked on over. "Hey there. How's it goin'?"

Bobbie Lee nodded. He was wearing a baseball cap, plain black with dark sunglasses. He nodded.

"I don't need a menu."

She smiled. "Great. I like a man who knows what he wants." He ignored her flirtatious eyes. Perhaps on another day, but ... he was on business and couldn't be sidetracked.

"I'll take the Tiny Yokum's burger with fries. Make the meat a little rare in the middle."

The lady was on the tall side, blonde hair and had some pretty good curves for a yooper woman. "Anything to drink?"

"Yeah, give me a bottle of Killians. Make sure its extra cold, please."

She nodded as she wrote down the order. "So ya wanna add the salad bar fer five ninety-nine?"

Bobbie Lee smirked. "Not in the yoo pee in the dead of winter." The waitress glanced around as if to make sure no one was listening.

"That's probably a good call. The lettuce is none too fresh these days."

She waited a moment, but Bobbie Lee looked away, continuing to ignore her. The waitress left so Bobbie Lee looked around to see what had changed. Printed on the menu to his right it said "Seafood, Steaks'n So Forth since '66." Nothing much ever changes in these small towns, and he liked that. Bobbie Lee liked things predictable. He started to read some of the signs near the top of the wall. One said "Upper Slobbovia" while another said "Good is better than evil cuz its nicer."

Bobbie Lee smiled. Good is definitely nicer, but that didn't necessarily make it any better. For fifteen minutes he went over plans in his mind. He was going to kill Jack Ruger and anyone else the man loved, as many as he could, actually, and in the most heinous way possible. It wasn't really necessary, and probably the smart play would be to drive on up to Canada for a while, but ... Bobbie Lee reached up with his left hand and stroked his whiskered chin. He was growing out a beard to make it harder for people to recognize him. A few hours ago he'd purchased a laptop and some other computer gear at Walmart. He'd already accessed the tax and real estate records for the county, so he knew exactly where Jack Ruger lived now, when he'd bought the property and what improvements he'd made to it. And thanks to Google Earth, he even knew what the man's house and property looked like from a satellite. Bobbie Lee had embraced technology and used it when ever possible, as it made him more efficient and productive in his job.

The waitress finally came back with his food, just as he was growing impatient. She set down the beer first and then the plate of food.

"I waited on the beer, so you could have it really cold with your meal."

Bobbie Lee nodded. "Thanks. I appreciate that."

She straightened up and stood there looking at him for a moment. Bobbie Lee said nothing to her. He just picked up his burger and took a bite.

"Pretty good, huh?"

He took a look at the meat inside and saw that it was perfect. "It'll do. Thanks."

"So is there anything else I can get ya?"

"Nope."

She nodded and then walked away. Bobbie Lee returned to his food. He picked up the bottle of catsup, twisted off the top and then dumped a large spot of it on his plate. He had to hurry up and eat the fries while they were still hot. Cold fries were about as putrid as warm Mountain Dew on a summer's day.

About halfway through his meal, Bobbie Lee glanced up

and saw the cop walk in through the back door. He kept eating, but watched where he sat down. It was too close for comfort. Bobbie Lee picked up the pace a bit. He should have gotten another drive-through burger, but he was getting sick of take-out, and he seldom got to Munising. He thought to himself as he ate *Just too many damn cops in this town.*

That's when he noticed the cop looking in his direction. He was a city cop, and this was not exactly the height of tourist season, so he would undoubtedly stick out more than usual.

That was enough for Bobbie Lee. He quickly finished his burger, and left the rest of his fries on the plate. He still didn't have the check, so he pulled out his wallet and plopped a twenty down on the table. Then he got up and walked past the cop without looking in his direction.

When he got outside he breathed a sigh of relief. Then he looked over at Daisy Mae and called out to her again. "See ya later, chickie!"

That's when he heard the door open behind him. He forced himself to not turn around. He knew who it was, so he continued walking to his truck.

"Excuse me, sir! I need to speak with you a moment."

Bobbie Lee glanced over his shoulder and then stopped walking. "Yes, officer?"

Bobbie Lee saw the cop's hand resting on the grip of his Glock. He hated Glocks. "May I see some identification, sir?"

Bobbie Lee smiled innocently. He was about two feet from the corner of the building, and he was pretty sure it would stop a bullet. "It's right here in my back pocket." He reached back slowly, taking half a step to his left toward the wall, trying to make it seem like the most normal thing in the world. The cop watched him closely, not letting down his guard even a little. He was only six feet away from Bobbie Lee now. Instead of pulling out his wallet, Bobbie Lee canted his body away from the police officer so he couldn't see the gun in the five o'clock position inside Bobbie Lee's waistband. He pulled the pistol out smoothly and swiftly as he continued to move to the left.

The cop started his draw as well, but Bobbie Lee was safely behind the corner of the building before the cop could bring his gun up. Because only Bobbie Lee's head was exposed, the cop had to aim, whereas all Bobby Lee had to do was press the trigger. He shot five times into the cop's upper chest before the man went down to the pavement. He closed the distance and then looked down at the cop, wheezing on the ground. One shot had gone high and missed the top of the cop's body armor. while the others had been absorbed by the Kevlar. The policeman tried to raise his gun, but didn't quite have the strength yet. Bobbie Lee looked into the man's blue eyes and raised his gun up and pressed the trigger.

Bobbie Lee reached back and placed the gun back into his inside-the-waistband holster. He then glanced around the parking lot, and then up at the roof line where he saw the surveillance camera staring down on him. He looked into the camera and smiled. Then he took off his hat and glasses. Bobbie Lee winked and blew a kiss before mouthing the words "I'm coming, Jack."

Almost as an afterthought, he reached down and removed the Taser from the cop's duty belt. And then Bobbie Lee turned and walked away.

CHAPTER 12

<u>*Sunday, 4PM - Flo's Diner, Jackpine*</u>

"**Y**OU GOTTA GIT OUTTA HERE, girl. Don't be here when Jack gits back. There's no tellin' what he might do."

Amanda tightened her brow and looked off into the empty dining room. "I'm not leaving, Flo, and he can't make me go! What's he going to do, put me in jail?"

Florence didn't like the determined sound of her voice. They'd been debating this topic off and on for hours now, and Florence was losing patience with the young woman. "Now, girl, that's gotta be the most stubborn and mule-headed thing ya done ever said. Now there's a killer on the loose 'n he's comin' ta kill Jack. So if ya really care 'bout 'em, then ya best be gettin' yer pretty, lil tail on back ta New York City. Ya here me?"

Amanda watched the snowfall increase outside as the light faded from the sky. It always seemed to snow more here during the night-time hours. She didn't want to leave, at least not yet. She still hadn't found Sara Sinai, and she'd lose her job for sure if she dared return to New York without a signed contract. Her boss had made that much pretty clear to her. And then there was the question of Jack Ruger. She didn't know how she felt about him right now. Deep inside she was just a jumble of mixed-up emotions that she couldn't seem to separate. She tried to think it through logically, but, there was something blocking that part of her brain.

"Yer not thinkin' clear right now, darlin.'" Florence hesitated before going on, as if she was still trying to sort it all out herself. "Listen, sweetie, I was here when Jack went through this before, when he done hunted this guy down 'n tried ta kill 'em. I was glad fer that cuz Fred was my brother, but ... I just got a bad feelin' 'bout this one. Like ... I don't know ... like Jack might have a tougher go of it this time round."

Amanda listened to her every word, even though she didn't like what she was saying. "Maybe, Flo. I don't know."

"Just head back ta L'Anse, ta the motel 'n you kin figure it out there." And then she added."I promise ta call ya soon as somethin' happens. Ya got my word."

Amanda thought about it for a moment. In her heart, she didn't want to go. But her head was telling her it was the right thing to do.

"They got Wi-Fi there ... an good cell service."

Florence reached over and put her right hand on Amanda's back. There was just something about the way she touched her, that made Amanda feel like a child, like she was being loved and comforted. Finally, Amanda reluctantly gave in.

"Okay. I'll go to the motel and wait there until tomorrow. But you have to call me as soon as you know something."

Florence smiled and gave the other woman a hug. "Ya know I will, girl. But ya best git along real quick, cuz it's a gettin' dark out, an there's another storm kickin' up. I don't want ya gettin' stuck in a blizzard."

Amanda thought about it for a few more seconds, and then she nodded and started to put her coat on. Florence rushed back to the kitchen and filled up a brown paper sack with pasties and brought it back to her.

"I just now made 'em 'n they're still warm. Best pasties in da yoo pee, girl."

Amanda had never eaten a pasty, wasn't even sure what

they were, but she hugged Florence quickly, took the bag and headed out the door. The bell over the door rang out as she left. She took one last look at the diner and then headed to her car, all the while glancing around nervously, looking for a bad guy behind every tree and a killer concealed in every shadow. The early evening twilight scared her more than usual, and she suddenly found herself eager to leave Jackpine.

Inside the diner, Florence picked up the land line and punched in Jack's number. It rang once before he answered.

"She just headed out, Jack."

"Are you sure?"

Florence nodded as she answered him.

"Course I'm sure, Jack. Just watched her headlights drive away. She'll be in L'Anse in no time flat."

Jack breathed a sigh of relief. "Good. Now I can focus on my work." There was a pause. "Flo, do I need to worry about you at all?"

Florence reached down into her apron pocket and placed her hand on the steel revolver. "Nope. I kin take care of myself. I'm just gonna lock up here, 'n pass out the rest a those wanted flyers 'n then git back to my house. I'll be okay. Don't worry."

Jack smiled softly. "Thank you Flo."

Jack hung up the phone and then grabbed his coat off the back of his chair. It was time to get ready. It just wouldn't be friendly to not give the man a proper greeting when he finally got here. After all, he'd come a long way and went through a lot of trouble to get here. And Jack had no intention of being caught off guard.

Sunday, 5PM - Four Miles South of Jackpine

By the time Amanda drove out of Jackpine, the sun was going down quickly and the wind had kicked up, driving down and around, swirling like a wounded leopard. Snow came down hard now, flying through the air almost parallel to the ground. As the snow crossed her headlights, the whiteness of it illuminated and almost blinded her. She quickly learned that keeping her headlights on dim was the only way to see the road. However, this limited her visibility and she could see only a few yards in front of the car. Amanda drove very little in New York City, so these conditions were unknown to her, and, quite frankly, she didn't know how to drive on the snowy roads, when to brake, how to brake, and when and how to turn the wheel. So when the deer ran out in front of her car, it was almost a certainty that she would slam on her brakes and cut the steering wheel hard to the right in an effort to avoid it. This. of course, sent her car into an uncontrolled slide off the road, down the embankment and into a pine tree.

For some reason unknown, the air bag failed to deploy and Amanda's forehead hit the steering wheel hard. She felt the impact, then a strong pain in her forehead. Just before she lost consciousness, she felt the blood running down and into her eyes. And then, her last thought was of Jack Ruger, the tall, dark, handsome man, strong and capable, one who had already saved her once. *Jack, help. Where are you?*

An hour later Amanda regained consciousness. She opened her eyes and saw nothing but a sheet of white on her windshield and all the other windows. Her head was aching more now than it had yesterday, but she forced herself to focus as she desperately tried to clear the cobwebs from her head. Listening carefully, she could tell the car was no longer running, and that the wind was blowing at gale force outside.

She thought back and remembered the deer running in front of her, slamming on the brakes and then the fast descent down the embankment before the sudden stop. That was all she could remember. Every time she moved her head, it made her nauseous and she almost threw up. Amanda looked down for her phone on the console, but it had slid down onto the floor. As slowly and carefully as she could, she unbuckled her seat belt and lowered herself down to the phone. Their was also a sharp pain in her left collarbone when she moved, so she assumed it was broken.

Upon retrieving the cell phone, she was disappointed to learn she had no service. She tried calling Jack anyway, but it wouldn't go through. Amanda did a quick surveillance of her hips and legs and found no other injuries. She was really starting to hate Jackpine.

She looked at the clock on her phone and saw that it was just past 6PM, which meant she'd been out for quite a while. The car was already getting pretty cold inside. Then it occurred to her. *I can send Jack a text. That requires less of a signal.* So she quickly picked up her phone and typed out a message.

> *Jack, I'm hurt. Car accident. About four miles south of town. Car down embankment. Will try to get up to road and walk back to town. It's 6PM. Sorry I'm such a pain. Amanda*

She pressed send, but it didn't go anywhere. The phone just seemed to lock up. The snow was howling outside, and she was getting colder by the minute. Amanda had no idea what the smart play was in this situation. Would she freeze to death in the car? Should she walk back to town? In the end she decided to get out and walk. *How bad could it be?* She tucked her cell phone into her coat pocket.

Amanda forced the door open and the wind and cold immediately rushed in along with blowing snow. When she stepped out into the night, her feet sunk up to her knees in a snow drift. She couldn't see more than ten feet in front of her, but she knew the road was up the embankment, so she started climbing up. It took her ten minutes to get back up to the road, which was now covered in a foot of snow. At first she wasn't sure if it really was the road, but then she saw the yellow road sign signifying a curve ahead.

Her leather designer jacket had cost her more than a thousand dollars, but right now she'd trade it for a thirty-dollar parka and a three-dollar stocking cap on the clearance rack at Walmart. Her shoes were low-cut, fine, top-grain kid skin, and were almost worthless in the snow. She fell down several times while standing in the road.

That was when Amanda realized she'd made a mistake ... perhaps the last mistake of her life. She should've stayed with the car and waited for rescue. After just ten minutes in the storm, she could no longer feel her feet or her face. She turned back down the hill, but couldn't see anything. If she tried to return to the car and missed it by even a few feet ... She didn't want to think about it. Amanda's heart sank. She was going to die.

And then she heard the sound of the engine, and a spark of hope flared up inside her. *It was Jack! It had to be Jack!* It gradually got closer and closer, and Amanda didn't think to step out of the middle of the road. She was too cold to think. She just knew that help was here and she would live again.

The truck pulled to a stop just before hitting her and Amanda walked to the driver's side window. The power window slowly came down and the man asked her the obvious question.

"You need a ride, lady?"

Amanda was disappointed that it wasn't Jack, but that feeling quickly went away and was replaced by elation. *She wasn't going to die!*

"Oh, thank god you're here. Can I get a ride into Jackpine?" Her words came out a little unclear because her lips and cheeks were frozen, but it was good enough so that he could understand her.

The man nodded. She couldn't see his eyes through the dark glasses he was wearing.

"Sure thing, lady. Climb on in."

Amanda's heart was brimming with joy when she opened the passenger-side door and crawled into the warm truck cab. She extended her frozen right hand over to her rescuer in gratitude.

"My name's Amanda."

At first he just looked at her, but then he took off his sunglasses and let her see his eyes. And that's when Amanda recognized him. Her heart filled with terror as he reached over with his right hand.

"Name's Bobbie. Glad I could help you."

7PM, the House that Jack Built

Jack Ruger put down his screw gun and took one last look at the surveillance camera that he'd just mounted on the ceiling of his great room. He got down off the stepladder and sat down in the wooden rocker beside the fireplace. It was a massive fireplace, made of large granite stones the size of basketballs. Jack loved anything rustic, so he'd patterned the house after buildings he'd seen while visiting Yellowstone National Park. Carrie had helped him to design it, and they were to live in it together after their marriage. But that wouldn't happen now.

The walls and ceilings were mostly made of knotty pine planking, while the floors were solid oak, shiny and new. He'd used field stones to accent the base of the walls. The fireplace was built in the center of the room, and stood a full six feet in height, then it tapered gradually until it reached the ceiling. The mantle was six inches thick and six feet wide, made of red oak he'd cut down and planed from this very property. In fact, most of the materials, the wood and stone at least, had come from Jack's forty-acre parcel.

He'd already set up the wireless base station and mounted all the surveillance cameras, and was now ready to start with the door and window alarms. He went back to the garage and started taking the alarms, still in their boxes, back into the house. This security system was something he'd had in his garage for over a year now, but had never gotten around to installing. He just hadn't seen the need, what with Jackpine being so tame these days. But now, with Bobbie Lee on the loose, he figured it was now or never.

Jack had always been an orderly man, so he arranged the boxes according to their kind and set them in rows, being careful to maintain military alignment. For the next three hours he installed the alarms, then tested them for functionality. Everything worked fine. He spent another two hours installing the motion sensor alarms before finally running out of energy. He was totally exhausted.

In the morning, he'd install the glass breakage sensors and then the smoke and heat sensors. He was just too tired to do any more work tonight.

He looked outside at the snow pouring down in an almost white sheet. Then he stepped out onto the deck to look outside. There was already twelve inches of freshly fallen snow on the deck planks, and he couldn't see farther than ten feet into his back yard. He suddenly thought of Amanda, hoping that she'd made it to L'Anse before the storm hit. Jack stepped back inside and pulled his cell phone out of his back pocket. No signal.

He walked into the kitchen and picked up the land line and dialed Amanda's cell number. After a few rings, the call went to voice mail. Jack cleared his throat while he waited for the beep.

"Oh, Hi, ah ... Amanda. Hi. I was just making sure you made it to the motel okay before the storm hit." He waited a few seconds, trying to think of something else to say. "And, just wanted to apologize for being so grumpy with you. Things are a little bit tense around here right now." He paused. "I just don't want you to get hurt on account of me." Jack looked over at the fireplace and saw that it was dying down. "Anyways, I'll try calling again in the morning. Maybe you'll have service by then. Bye."

Jack hung up the phone and then walked over to the fire. He opened the glass and picked up the steel poker to move the coals around. Then he set it down and selected a large oak log for the night. He put two more oak blocks into the fire and closed it back up before adjusting the damper for the night.

He stood there and stared at the flames as they started to catch and then suddenly roared back to life. He watched the yellow sprigs of fire lap up hungrily at the fresh oak blocks. They would be totally consumed by morning, nothing but red-hot coals. Jack felt that way sometimes, like he'd been burning bright for a long time, and he was now totally used up, all burned and good for nothing more than to be thrown outside on the ash heap.

Jack shook his head. That was useless thinking. He whispered a little prayer for Amanda and then another one for Flo. He decided to sleep on the couch tonight closer to the fireplace. It would be warmer, and he could hear the land line better if anyone needed help. He got a comforter out of the closet and plopped himself down on the couch. He looked at the flames again, letting the licking fire hypnotize him into a gentle daze. But, just before falling off to sleep, Jack reached his right hand down to his Walther Q5 and touched it, just to make sure it was still there if he needed it.

CHAPTER 13

BOBBIE LEE CARRIED THE WOMAN'S body into the modest summer home of some rich business man from Chicago or Detroit, or perhaps even Milwaukee. He dumped her down onto the floor and then flexed the muscles in his arms. He needed to work out more. One should never let one's self get out of shape.

He looked down at Amanda and smiled. He would be here at this cottage until the storm blew over and the roads were plowed. This woman would be his entertainment for a few days, at least until he tired of her. By then he'd be ready to take care of his final loose end.

Bobbie Lee rolled Amanda over and pulled off her leather jacket, all the while wondering *What were you doing out in that storm dressed like this?* And that got him to thinking that she wasn't from around here, and that he needed to check her wallet. But first he had to make sure she didn't go anywhere, so he quickly brought out a roll of heavy-duty duct tape and secured her hands and feet.

After that, he went to the basement and turned on the furnace. As he was doing that, he wondered why more people didn't install security systems. They weren't that expensive or difficult. You just had to do it. But so many people were trusting, convinced that nothing bad would ever happen to them, and that mistaken belief allowed Bobbie Lee to do many of the things he did. He'd checked out three other summer homes before deciding on this one, simply because the others had security systems and this one did not.

Once back upstairs in the bedroom, he picked up the lady's jacket and emptied the pockets onto the bed. When he saw the cell phone, something akin to fear surged into his body. Cops could do a lot with a cell phone signal these days. He knew several guys in the joint who'd been captured and convicted based on cell phones, and he didn't want that to happen to him. Technology was a sword that cut both ways.

Bobbie Lee quickly picked it up and pressed the button. It looked like an iPhone 8 or something close to it. He'd read an article about them online. Fortunately, the phone hadn't powered off yet, so it didn't need the password. But he would need the touch ID. He'd never understood why prisons allowed criminals like him access to a world of information via the internet. Most inmates he knew spent their time learning better ways to rob and kill people while in prison, using computers supplied to them by the ones who were supposed to be rehabilitating them.

He crawled down onto the carpet where the woman was lying, rolled her over onto her stomach to better get at her hands. Bobbie Lee took the thumb of her right hand and placed it on the touch button. Nothing. It took several tries, but the phone eventually unlocked. *Man, this woman has a lot of apps.* He was relieved to see she had no service. That would lessen the chances that the police could locate her phone, but he'd need to get rid of it nonetheless as it was just too big a risk to take for no benefit.

Bobbie Lee opened her email app and scanned through some of the messages. He quickly learned she was from New York City and worked at a place called Bedrock Publishing. Then he opened her message app and was stunned to read the following message:

Jack, I'm hurt. Car accident. About four miles south of town. Car down embankment. Will try to get up to road and walk back to town. It's 6PM. Sorry I'm such a pain. Amanda

And then he smiled. So the woman knew a man named Jack? Could this be his Jack ... Jack Ruger, the man he'd love to torture and kill more than any person on the planet? He saw that the message delivery had failed and felt relieved. But still ... he needed to get the phone away from him. A cell phone could ping a cell tower at any given time, especially after this storm let up. He could just destroy the phone, but if the phone had pinged a tower recently, they would trace the signal right here. He needed to take the cell phone to another place away from here to throw them off his trail.

Bobbie Lee sighed, concluding that he'd have to go back out into the storm, and that's when he suddenly realized that crime was a lot of work. And then he thought of the million dollars he'd be digging up in a few days and knew that crime really does pay. It pays a lot!

Monday, 6AM - Jack's House

THE PHONE KEPT RINGING, BUT JACK HADN'T QUITE made the connection. He was deep inside a dream, a terrible dream and a lovely dream. He was beside Carrie's bed in the hospital and she was saying good bye to him again.

"I want you to be happy, Jack, but I know how you are." Her voice was weak, barely audible, so Jack had to move closer to hear her. "You are so loyal to me that, if I let you, you'll spend the rest of your life grieving my loss, and I don't want you to do that. I want you to be happy, Jack. I want you to have a good life."

Jack squeezed her hand and tried desperately not to cry, but it was just too hard. "I ... I can't, Carrie. I love you too much. I won't let you go."

Carrie smiled, emaciated in her bed, just a waif of her former self. In life she'd been a strong woman, both in body and soul, but here, now, on the threshold of her passing, Carrie Parker had all she could do just to breathe and speak her final words. Jack reached his left hand down to stroke her forehead. The chemo had taken away her beautiful, long, blonde hair, and she stared out at Jack now, lovingly, at her best, doing her utmost to be strong for him. She didn't want to go, but ... she had no choice, was being called home. And her next words were painful to speak, and they held on to her throat before leaving her mouth with barbed talons.

"Get married and have children, Jack. You are going to be such a great father. Give the love you have for me to another woman."

Jack could hold it back no longer and cried aloud. "No, I can't. Don't go."

Carrie smiled softly. She was fading now. "Take care of Jackpine for me, my love."

The phone kept ringing, but Jack kept pushing it to the back of his mind.

"I love you, Jack. You will always be my ... forever love."

The phone rang again and Jack woke up crying once more. He both hated and loved that dream, and this was the third night in a row for it. Jack felt exhausted. The land line was still ringing. Jack got up and walked wearily over to it.

"Jack Ruger here."

The man on the other end was terse and business like. "Chief Ruger, this is Chief Blaine from Munising."

Jack remembered meeting him at a conference a few years ago.

"You'll also be getting a call from the state police but that probably won't be until later this morning." He paused.

"Okay, what can I help you with, Chief Blaine?"

"Listen, Jack, there's something you need to know. One of my officers was murdered here yesterday by a man you know. Bobbie Lee Harper. He had a message for you, and

I've emailed it to you." He waited for Jack to say something, but there was nothing but silence, so Chief Blaine continued. "You're in great danger, Chief Ruger."

Jack suddenly realized he'd been holding his breath for the last ten seconds. He let out an audible sigh.

"Yes, I know. I'm preparing for him now." Jack looked out the window of the great room. The snow storm had stopped. And then Jack regained his sense of decorum.

"I'm sorry for your loss, Chief Blaine. Very sorry. I know what it's like to lose a brother."

The Munising police chief was silent for a moment. Jack just waited for him.

"Thanks chief. He was a good man. He left a wife and three kids."

Tears welled up in Jack's eyes, but he did his best to hold it back.

"Thanks for the info, chief. I'll look at the email right away."

Jack started to move the phone away from his ear, but Chief Blaine wasn't quite finished.

"Jack?"

"Yes, chief."

There was a powerful moment of silence.

"I want you to kill that son of a bitch!"

Jack's voice was tense and serious when he responded. "Count on it, Chief Blaine. I'll do what needs doing."

And then both men hung up.

Jack attended to the fireplace, dressed quickly and then double-checked to make sure the security system was working properly. He warmed up his SUV and drove into town. The snowplows had just been through, so it was easy driving. He saw that Paul Butler had already been here to plow out his own driveway. Paul made a good living up here in the winter.

As soon as he reached the edge of Jackpine, his cell phone chimed. Jack pulled into the police department and parked. He looked around cautiously and then back down at the phone.

He pulled up the message and his heart sank.

Jack, I'm hurt. Car accident. About four miles south of town. Car down embankment. Will try to get up to road and walk back to town. It's 6PM. Sorry I'm such a pain. Amanda

The email from Chief Blaine could wait. He quickly called Amanda's cell phone. It rang a few times before Jack noticed music playing up near the door of his office. It sounded like the melody to a song he didn't recognize. Jack put the cell phone in his jacket pocket and drew his pistol, holding it out in front of him as he moved stealthily toward the door. When he was still a few feet away, he saw the cell phone propped up on the window sill, playing some kind of modern music that sounded terrible to Jack. He lowered his handgun and reholstered. Then he took out his cell phone and disconnected the call to Amanda's phone. The music stopped instantly.

Jack sat at the counter, staring passively at the cell phone lying in front of him. Technically, it might be held as evidence later on if a crime had been committed. But right now, there was no reason to believe foul play had occurred. At least that's what the county sheriff thought. But Jack knew better. Amanda Walker was more than missing and Bobbie Lee Harper must be involved. How else could he explain the cell phone getting from four miles outside town all the way to the township office?

Monday, Noon - Jackpine Diner

JACK KNEW HOW AMANDA WAS DRESSED, THAT SHE HAD no real survival skills, and the likelihood of her surviving a four-mile walk in a freezing blizzard was low to nil.

"Jack, I done called her last night and again at seven this mornin' but she don't answer. I called the motel desk and they said she never got there."

Jack ran his fingers through his short hair and propped both his elbows up onto the counter. "I know that, Flo. We found her car on the side of the road four miles south of town."

Florence knew what she wanted to ask him, but didn't quite know how to phrase it, so she just blurted it out.

"Was there any blood in the car?"

Jack stopped running his hand through his hair as if he'd just been stabbed with a knife. "No ... well, there was a little on the steering wheel. But she said she was hurt when she texted me at six last night, so we expect a little bit of blood."

Jack blew on his coffee and took a little sip. "She's still alive, Flo. I can sense it."

Florence wiped her hands on her dirty apron. "Course she's still alive, Jack. Yer gonna find 'er too."

Jack put his head in both his hands and rubbed his temples. "Is this my fault, Flo? I'm the one who made her go home last night."

Florence leaned down closer to him from the other side of the counter. "Stop it, Jack! You did this with Carrie too 'n it's stupid! It ain't yer fault Carrie got cancer any more 'n it's yer fault Amanda got ... well, whatever happened to 'er."

Jack didn't say anything for a moment. He was thinking deeply, analyzing the information they had.

"Bobbie Lee has her, Flo. It's the only thing that adds up."

Florence took out her wet dish rag and started wiping off the counter even though it wasn't dirty. "Ya don't know that Jack. Sides, Bobbie Lee don't know Amanda even exists. Just a few days ago she was in New York City."

Jack took another sip of coffee. "I know that, Flo. It could just be a case of really bad luck. He was coming here anyways, so he could've seen her drive off the road and stopped to help."

But then Florence made a really good point. "Why would a killer an bank robber who done just escaped from prison stop 'n help somebody?"

Jack nodded. "Your right, Flo. He wouldn't stop to help, but ... he might stop for other reasons, now wouldn't he?"

Florence stopped wiping the counter and sucked in a big

breath. But she didn't say anything.

Just then Amanda's phone started to play that strange ring tone again. Jack and Florence both looked down at it. Jack pursed his lips together.

"Ya gonna answer it, Jack?"

Jack reached down with his right hand and picked it up. The screen was lit and it said "Slide to answer" Jack slid the screen to his right and then held it up to his ear. There was a moment of silence before he heard an ominous voice.

"Hi Jack. I told you we'd meet again."

CHAPTER 14

"**W**HAT'S WRONG, JACK? CAT got yer tongue? No more smart, tough-guy cop remarks?"

Jack Ruger listened to Bobbie Lee taunting him, but he truly had nothing worthwhile to say. But he had to say something, so he spewed out the first thought that crossed his mind.

"I should have killed you when I had the chance."

Bobbie Lee laughed out loud, and it sent a chill down Jack's spine. "Yes, you should have killed me. But you didn't, so here I am." He waited for Jack to respond, but Jack said nothing. "As I recall you did your best to kill me that first time around, Jack, but you didn't. And I have a bullet lodged a half inch away from my heart as evidence. They never took it out, Jack. They said the operation was too risky, that it would probably kill me. So, for the rest of my life I have a constant heaviness on my heart, a perpetual reminder that you bested me in a fair fight, Jack. And I don't like that."

Jack tried hard to steady his breathing. Initially he'd been afraid upon hearing Bobbie Lee's voice, but that emotion was gone now, replaced first by anger, and then sheer, visceral animal rage.

"Just tell me where you are, Bobbie Lee. I'll clear my

schedule and we can have do lunch. Then after that we can have that rematch you've been wanting for so long."

Bobbie Lee laughed again. "You're right, Jack. I have been wanting a rematch, but this time I'll be the one calling the shots, no pun intended."

Jack worked hard to master his anger before responding. "Well, Bobbie Lee, I wouldn't want to disappoint you on that one. After all, you are a visitor to Jackpine, and I wouldn't want to be rude. We've always prided ourselves in our country hospitality up here in the frozen north."

"Yes, I know. It's the kind of hospitality that hunts a man down and tries to kill him."

Florence was surprised to see Jack suddenly smile. She didn't say anything, but she wanted so much to hear the conversation.

"Well now, Bobbie Lee, you did shoot my foster parents. You shot Fred in the back and then in the head. I'd say that entitles me to a little payback, don't you think?"

Bobbie Lee nodded and smiled. "Yes, I suppose it does. But I want you to know something, Jack. Your father didn't beg for his life at the end. It didn't matter. I was going to kill him anyways. But I've always been impressed by his courage. He wasn't afraid to die. He did beg for your mom's life though, and I considered his request ... for a half a second. I wasn't going to kill her until he tried to pressure me into sparing her. So it was really his own fault that she died."

There was a pause. Jack didn't trust himself to respond.

"So I shot her in the leg, and then in the arm, and then in the head. I wanted Fred to watch and hear her suffer. I enjoyed his screams. It was orgasmic in a way."

Finally Jack spoke, in a low guttural spewing.

"I'm going for the head shot, Bobbie Lee."

Bobbie Lee laughed out loud. "I would expect no less of you Jack. In fact, I'd be disappointed if you didn't hate me. I want you to promise to do your best to kill me, Jack. I want nothing less than your best on this one. Promise me right now that you'll do your best to kill me."

"Let me talk to Amanda first. I want to hear her voice."

Bobbie Lee's laugh was loud and unrestrained. "Oh, Jack. I just knew that our first talk was going to be the most satisfying of my entire life!"

"So let me talk to her. I need to know she's still alive."

Bobbie Lee was silent for just a moment. When he spoke again all humor was gone from his voice and replaced by malice and hate.

"No, Jack. You can't talk to her. You already know I have her and that she's still alive. And you know this because you know me. You know that I'm not done using her yet. I was just going to rape her repeatedly and then kill her, but ... then I found out she was your special friend. So, of course, that changed things. Yes, I'll keep her alive, but just so long as you cooperate and do as I say. I like control, Jack. I always have. And you know that. So long as you do what I want, then I'll let her live and I won't abuse her. But ... disobey me even once, and she will suffer the likes of pain that no one on this earth has ever experienced. So, I'll ask you one more time. Promise me, Jack, that you'll do your very best to kill me."

Jack squeezed the cell phone harder, almost hard enough to break it. "I promise. Just tell me where to meet you, Bobbie Lee. All I need is a time and a place."

There was a moment of silence. "I'll get back to you on that one. Good bye for now, Jack." And then the line went dead.

Monday, 12:10PM - Jackpine Diner

Upon hanging up Jack immediately called the county sheriff's office and brought them up to speed on his phone call with Bobbie Lee Harper. The sheriff's office then filled out an exigency request form in lieu of obtaining a search warrant, citing exigent circumstances. This was much faster than contacting a judge to get a formal search warrant.

This was presented to the phone service provider who then pinged Bobbie Lee's cell phone in an attempt to locate his position within an accuracy of just a few yards.

An hour later the sheriff called back with the results."Hi Jack Sheriff Gonzales here. We came up blank on the ping, at least so far. But right now it's looking like he destroyed the phone right after he made the call."

Jack was seated in his office behind his desk and let out an aggravated sigh. "I'm not surprised, Jeff. Bobbie Lee's no dummy."

"You got that right. I have his psychological profile and prison records here on my desk. I know you've already seen it, but this guy is a handful. He's not going to be an easy one, Jack. I know he's close by, but he knows we're hunting him."

Jack leaned back in his chair and it creaked loudly. "I agree. He probably has a whole bunch of throwaway phones. He'll use them once and then toss 'em."

There was a moment of silence. "Jack, I don't want you to get discouraged. I've called in extra reserve deputies and we've got all the main roads covered. The state police are also bringing in extra people. This guy made the mistake of killing a cop, so he's pretty high profile."

"Bobbie Lee made a lot of mistakes, Jeff, and the first one was to kill my foster parents."

The sheriff coughed on the other end of the line before answering. "Listen, Jack, don't make this personal. It'll cloud your judgement. Stay professional, and we'll work together and bring this guy in. Agreed?"

The sheriff sensed Jack's hesitation. "Jack? Are we agreed?"

Jack finally answered. "Yeah, Jeff. Agreed. I'll call you as soon as he contacts me."

They said good bye and Jack hung up the phone. He stared down at the land line on his desk, and then back at his cell phone beside it as if willing it to ring. But it just laid there, dead, inanimate, taunting him with silence.

Jack looked out the window and did a quick search of the parking lot. He knew there would be nothing there. Bobbie Lee was no dummy. He had a plan, an articulate and devious plan. He would study Jack and wait for the right moment. He would catch Jack alone, at a time and place of his own choosing, where only Bobbie Lee had the advantage, and then he would strike. It would be bold; it would be strong, and it would be overwhelming.

Jack had no misconceptions on this one. Before, he'd been hunting Bobbie Lee, but now ... there was no doubt. Bobbie Lee was hunting him.

Monday, 2PM - Twelve Miles from Jackpine

"So, LITTLE MISS PRETTY, HOW YOU FEELING TODAY?"

Amanda Walker lifted her head up and groaned. Her head felt like it was filled with magma and it was trying desperately to escape.

"Who ... who are you?"

Bobbie Lee smiled. "I think you already have a pretty good idea who I am, now don't ya sweetheart."

It was less painful to talk than to nod her head, so she spoke softly to him. "Yes, you're the guy who wants to kill Jack."

Bobbie Lee laughed out loud. "Yes, that's exactly right! In fact, you have completely defined me in one sentence. That is amazing ... truly amazing!"

Amanda lifted her head slowly to make eye contact and immediately regretted it. "You're a textbook sociopath."

Anger immediately flared up in Bobbie Lee's eyes and he yelled at the top of his lungs.

"Will you people get it right! I am not a sociopath! I'm a psychopath! If you're going to use terms, then you'd better get it right."

And then he appeared to calm down almost as quickly as he'd become angry. "Please, Ms. Walker. I am not a sociopath. A sociopath has a conscience and I do not. Now, it's true that neither of us can empathize with another human, though I've been known to fake it a time or too, when it was in my best interest of course." His eyes were smiling again, but it wasn't a happy smile; it was the smile of a man who'd shed too much blood and who enjoyed it immensely.

"In fact, if you want to get technical about it, clinical workers never diagnose someone as a sociopath or as a psychopath. The correct diagnosis would be antisocial personality disorder. I mean, let's face it, if anyone should know about clinical diagnoses it would be me. Do you have any idea how many times I've been poked and prodded and scanned and interrogated? Thank god they no longer allow shock therapy or I'd be a goner for sure."

Amanda's head hung down, with her chin resting on her chest. She couldn't believe what she was hearing. *Did he really think like this?*

"How many people have you killed?"

Bobbie Lee's face beamed happily. He seemed to enjoy talking about himself. "At first I didn't keep track, but then I realized that statistics are important in murder just as much as they are in say professional football. Among football enthusiasts, it's common knowledge that Adam Vinatieri is the NFL's all-time leading scorer. They make game cards out of things like that and kids and adults collect them. I think it would be great if they put my face on a collector's card. I could get 10 points for a murder, 5 points for attempted murder, 3 for armed robbery, maybe 2 for rape. Wouldn't that be great?"

Amanda thought it odd that he put a higher value on armed robbery than he did rape. She didn't know how to answer him, so she just nodded her head softly to hold down the pain. So long as he was talking, he wasn't hurting her.

"So how many points would that make for you, Bobbie Lee?"

Bobbie Lee cocked his head to one side and thought. He was quiet for over a minute, and Amanda was careful not to disturb him. Finally he spoke.

"Ya know, come to think of it, I'm not rightly sure, but it's gotta be in the thousands. Things just tend to add up over time, ya know what I mean?"

Amanda slowly nodded her head to minimize the pain. "So, how many points will I be worth?"

Bobbie Lee immediately smiled. "I like you, Ms Walker. I really do." And then he thought some more. "You probably won't like this, but you're going to be a lot of points for me. I hope you can appreciate the significance of that."

And then he seemed to become almost giddy. "I've already assaulted you, kidnapped you and you'll undoubtedly be raped several times, being as good looking as you are. I mean you can hardly begrudge me that. And then of course I'll torture you a bit, depending on how Jack behaves himself. But I want you to know that it's nothing personal. It's just part of the game. It's just business Amanda."

Amanda wanted to cry out loud, but she purposely concealed it. It would gain her nothing, and he might even enjoy it.

"Well, I appreciate you being up front with me, Bobbie Lee. Just because you're going to kill me, doesn't mean we can't be friends."

Bobbie Lee smiled. "Now that's the spirit!" And then he got up off his chair and put on his coat. "Listen, I've got business to take care of, so you just relax and I'll be back in a bit." He turned to walk away. "Is there anything I can get you while I'm out?"

Amanda thought for a minute, trying to decipher whether or not it was a serious question. She decided to play it safe.

"No, Bobbie Lee. But thanks for asking. I appreciate the sentiment."

Bobbie Lee smiled. I like you, Amanda. I really, really do." He turned to walk away.

"And don't wait up, darling, I may be a while."

The bedroom door closed behind him and Amanda was left alone with her fear, her hopelessness and her pain. She wondered where she was and what Jack was doing right now. She thought about praying for help, but suddenly felt very hypocritical about it. After all, she'd never prayed before, so why would God honor her request now?

And then she remembered the way Florence had prayed for her, and a gentle warmth came over her.

Hypocrite or not ... she decided to pray. After all, Jack was not coming for her. Jack couldn't hope to beat this man, and nothing short of a miracle could save her.

CHAPTER 15

Monday, 3PM - Jackpine Diner

JACK PULLED HIS **SUV** INTO THE diner and slammed it into park. Florence had just called him at his office, telling him that the local militia was having a meeting right now in her diner and they were armed to the teeth. Jack looked around the parking lot. It was filled with twenty or so vehicles, mostly trucks and four-wheel drive types. A few of them were even painted in camouflage. He already knew a lot of these people. Despite the bad press they got. they weren't a bad lot, not out to overthrow the government or anything like that. For the most part they were just law-abiding citizens who didn't like government overreach and they loved their guns. Boy did they love guns.

Jack sat out in the parking lot for a few minutes trying to think of a way to control the situation. He doubted they were breaking any laws, and, quite frankly, Flo could use the extra business. Jack came to a bold decision and got out of his vehicle and walked to the door. The bell overhead announced his arrival.

Jack stopped just inside and looked around. There were about forty people there, most of them men, dressed in camo, denim or wool coats. He'd never seen so many people inside Flo's diner before. All the chatter ceased as soon as people noticed him there. Jack took a look at the assortment of fire-arms in the room. Almost everyone had a pistol of some sort on their hip. He saw Glocks and Springfields and Smith and Wessons in all calibers, but most of them were big. He even saw a few single-action cowboy revolvers. One man had a confederate cap and ball pistol on his hip. There was also an assortment of long guns leaning up against every wall in the place. Most of them were AR15 types, but he also saw bolt action deer rifles, shotguns and even a few muzzle loaders.

He saw Florence motioning behind the counter for him. He took one last look around before speaking. Everyone was staring at him, some with blank looks, but others with open hostility. Jack kept it brief and non-threatening.

"Morning folks. Carry on. Don't let me interrupt your meal." He walked over to Florence and she beckoned him into the kitchen. She was beyond giddy.

"Would ya lookit all the customers, Jack. I'm gonna make dern near a fortune today! These guys eat like horses!"

Jack's eyes narrowed a bit. "So you're okay with them being in here, Flo? They're not causing you any trouble or anything?"

Florence laughed. "You kiddin' me. These guys er great tippers."

Jack smiled for the first time that day. "So the guns don't bother you at all?"

She laughed out loud and reached down into her apron pocket and pulled out her revolver. Jack noticed her finger was on the trigger and it was pointed at his leg, so he took a step back.

"Calm down, Flo. Finger off the trigger, please."

She put the gun back in her pocket again.

"So, Flo, if everything's okay, then why did you call me over here?"

Florence reached over and grabbed onto his left forearm. "Jack, these folks wanna help out. They wanna catch this Bobbie Lee fella 'n string 'em up."

Jack's face grew serious. "Well, Flo, I don't think lynching a man would be considered helping out, do you?"

Florence thought out loud. "Maybe they could do somethin' Jack. I mean ... Look at 'em. That's a lotta eyes 'n ears. Maybe you could use 'em somehow?"

Jack started to form his rebuttal, but ... then he got to thinking. Florence was right. If he left these people to their own devices, then they were bound to run afoul with the county deputies, the state boys and maybe even other civilians. But ... if he could harness their energy ... ?

He stepped away from Florence and moved back out into the diner. People saw him, and they all stopped talking one by one. Jack held up his hand to get their attention.

"Folks, Florence is telling me that you all are wanting to help out with this man hunt. Is that true?"

There was a general chorus of expletives in the affirmative, and even a few hearty amens.

"Well, now that's great, and I applaud you for your civic mindedness. Truth is we're in a bad way here and the law enforcement of Jackpine would be mighty grateful for your help."

A man near the counter stood up and faced him. "What'd y'all need, Jack?"

Jack recognized the man as Johnny Sterling and smiled politely. "Well, Johnny, the man we're looking for has already killed four people just in the last few days. He has a woman kidnapped. Her name is Amanda Walker. And some of you knew Fred Wentley, Flo's brother. This is the guy who killed Fred and his wife Irma years back. He's been in Marquette prison, but broke out a few days ago. We believe he's somewhere in or near Jackpine township. The state boys think he's driving a blue Chevy pick-up truck with a white cap on the back. I can even give you the license number."

He looked at all the men and women in the diner. He had their attention. "Now, this guy is heavily armed and extremely dangerous. If you see him you are not to approach him. You just call the dispatcher and they'll send units to help."

"Why can't we just shoot the bastard?"

Other people chimed in as well.

"Yeah, we got guns,'n he's the bad guy. Let's just shoot his ass!"

"Yeah we should kill 'em!"

"Shoot dat sumbish!"

Jack held his hands up to calm them down.

"Folks please. Just calm down. Now there's not a thing anyone can do unless we find him first. And the longer this man is free, the more people he'll kill. I have an idea that I think will help."

Everyone stopped talking and waited for Jack to explain.

"Most of you folks have lived here your whole lives, just like me. And you know every nook and cranny of this whole county. I want you to organize yourselves and do a systematic search of the entire township. Some of you can take the villages and the rest can search the countryside. I doubt you'll find him at a motel or a city. Besides, the county and state boys will be checking those places out."

He tried to make eye contact with as many people as he could as he talked. "But you folks have the edge out here in the country. You know where every vacant, house, farm and cottage in the township is located, and that's just the kind of place that Bobbie Lee would hole up in. He's using some place like that as a base of operations, and I'm guessing our one greatest hope of rescuing Amanda Walker is to find his hidey hole and then flush him out."

They started yelling again.

"Yeah! And then we kill 'em!"

"Kill the sumbish!

"Shoot 'em dead!"

"Yeah, we'll make 'em yoo pee dead!"

Johnny Sterling yelled as loud as he could and everyone shut up again. Johnny Sterling was six foot eight and 300 pounds. And when Johnny talked, people listened ... or else.

"I think what Jack's sayin' is we can't just go around like a mob tryin' to find a guy so we kin kill 'em. We got rules up here that gotta be followed." And then he looked Jack in the eyes. "So Jack, why don't you tell us when we can and when we can't shoot this guy."

The chief nodded his thanks and went on. "Good thinking, Johnny. I'm not saying you have to run away from him or that you have to let the guy shoot anyone else or that you can't defend yourself. You just have to follow the rules before using deadly force. I'm a cop and I have to do the same thing."

Florence brought Jack a cup of coffee in a white, glass mug. She set it down on the counter beside him. "Here in the great state of Michigan, you can use deadly force when either you or another innocent person is in reasonable fear of death or serious bodily injury or rape."

A man named Bobby Joe Napier stood up to talk, He wore a coonskin hat, and had a heavy yooper accent. "What da hell dat mean, eh?"

Johnny Sterling tried to clarify Jack's text book answer. "Bobbie Joe, that means if ya see 'em hurtin' someone ya'all kin kill 'em, but ya gotta see 'em doin' it. Right Jack?"

Jack nodded. "If he points a gun at you or another innocent person, then you are legally availed the use of deadly force."

Johnny Sterling nodded. "That means we kin kill 'em, right?"

Jack nodded again. "That's right, Johnny." He saw the coffee and reached down to pick it up. Then he turned to Johnny Sterling. "Johnny, can you organize these people into teams and send them out in a search pattern that covers the whole township? Make sure you don't trespass or damage anyone's property. Agreed?"

Johnny Sterling reached over and shook Jack's hand. "You got it, chief!"

And then he turned to Florence. "Flo, I want you to stop charging these good folks for their food and coffee. Just keep a running tab and I'll cover it."

Florence nodded her head. "Sure, Jack. If that's what you really want."

"And warm me up a bag of pasties. I'm gonna be out searching on my own."

"You want the pork 'n the beef like usual?"

"That'll do."

Jack started to mingle with the crowd, encouraging them and making friendly talk. He managed to talk a few of them down and to further clarify the legal use of deadly force.

Fifteen minutes later he left with a bag of pasties and a hot cup of coffee, all the while wondering, *what manner of force have I just unleashed on Bobbie Lee Harper?*

CHAPTER 16

J ACK PULLED HIS SUV AWAY FROM the diner and headed off down main street. He thought about going back to his office, but quickly dispatched that idea. There was no point. He would just sit there, staring absently at his desk, then the phone, then his desk again, and then maybe out the window.

Jack hated running in place, treading water, going nowhere fast. He hated it, but that's what he was relegated to do right now, because, he knew in his heart and in his mind that he was no longer in control. Bobbie Lee Harper was in control. It would be different if Jack knew where he was, but ... the word "if" was perhaps the biggest word in the universe, and certainly the nastiest and most frustrating of his life.

If Carrie hadn't died.

If Jack's aim had been better.

If Fred had survived.

If he knew where Bobbie Lee was.

"If" was a very tortuous word, oozing with self-pity and regret and he hated it.

But there was only one bottom line. He would continue to wait until his adversary was ready to fight, and there was nothing he could do to speed up the showdown.

And then it occurred to Jack, that there was something he

could do as he waited. He swung the SUV back around and a few miles later got on the road to the gravel pit.

By time he got there the sun, however weak, was already on the horizon, and clouds were moving in. Most people seldom target practiced at all, much less in the dead of winter with the wind howling and the freezing cold numbing his face and hands. But Jack was different. He practiced in all weather, the cold, the sleet, the heat, in the dark and in the night. Jack thought it ridiculous that most shooters restricted their shooting to the square range with only paper targets and no movement. And that's why he'd built his own range on his property. It was just a big bowl inside a gravel pit, but Jack practiced here every week.

Jack followed the plowed drive right out into the middle and parked beside a wooden table. He got out and opened the back of his SUV and quickly readied a thousand rounds of ammo, and his range bag. He smoothly unholstered his Q5, popped out the magazine, and racked the round out of the chamber. He then opened the plastic ammo box and took out five fully-loaded magazines. He slammed one of them into the well of his Q5 and chambered a round before reholstering. He put the remaining four mags into his coat pocket, causing the weight to make his jacket hang down on the left side.

Jack unzipped his fleece-lined leather jacket and stood beside his SUV, looking at the steel targets surrounding him. Some of the silhouettes were in close, no more than 12 feet away, while others were out to distances of 30 feet, 50 feet, 75, 100, 150, 200 feet and one even at 300 feet. Sometimes Jack even practiced with his handgun out to absurd distances of 150 yards and more. The odds of having to shoot from that distance were slim to none, but ... being accurate at a hundred yards ensured that he could hit anything he wanted at closer ranges. But then he added the elements of movement and stress.

Jack began to run in place, throwing up big chugs of steam out of his mouth and into the air around his head. Anyone driving by would have thought him a fool, but Jack didn't really care. This was how he stayed in shape, how he kept his edge. Jack ran in place for five minutes, and then he abruptly stopped, moved into his shooting stance as he drew his pistol, took aim and fired multiple rounds into each steel plate. Some plates got two rounds, others three or even four. Once a magazine was empty, Jack returned to running in place as he dropped the empty mag and replaced it with a fresh one. Then he dropped down and repeated the process. It didn't take long before all five magazines were lying in the snow in front of him.

Jack bent down to pick up the empty mags. His breathing was a bit labored and that bothered him. Jack was 36, but this was no time for old men. Both Amanda and Jackpine needed him to be at his best. And then he thought to himself, *I guess I need it for myself too.*

He returned to the open hatch of his SUV and quickly reloaded his five magazines. Then he walked back to his mark to repeat the drill. But this time he added real movement. It was tricky in the snow, but Jack ran to each steel target as quickly as possible, then stopped, fired multiple rounds, always a different number, and then ran again.

Jack was thankful that the thermometer had dropped to a mere 12 degrees, as cold snow was easier to move in than warm, wet snow. He could hear the snow scream under his boots as he moved. Wet snow was slippery and dangerous, but the colder the snow, the drier it was, and made for better traction.

Shots rang out in rapid succession, and very quickly those five mags were soon lying dead on the ground as well. Jack picked them up and started over. He repeated the drill until half his ammo was gone, then he converted to long range shooting. He started at 75 feet, firing quickly, about two shots per second. The steel target screamed back at him each time. Then he changed to the 100 foot target with the same process. Soon all his mags were empty again.

Jack reloaded and then worked on the 150 foot target with the same success, but his rhythm was starting to slow down now. Jack knew his limitations at longer ranges, knew that perfection was the goal, and that any rushed shot would result in nothing but dead air, no ringing of steel. And he hated that.

Jack quickly ammoed up again and went to work at the 200-foot range. His shots were slow and methodical, and every time he shot, the steel rang out. Jack always readjusted his grip before firing again. His rate of fire was only one round every two seconds, but jack seldom missed. When he did, he cursed silently and then redoubled his efforts. Jack found the smaller reticle on his red dot RMR sight to be extremely helpful in the fading light.

Jack could see the muzzle flash plainly now, and decided to shoot at the 300-foot steel while he could still see it plainly. From experience, Jack knew that his round would drop almost exactly 12 inches, that it would hit with the force of 253 foot pounds and a velocity of about 950 feet per second. Jack had never measured it himself, but according to the ballistics chart, the round would reach the target in exactly 293 milliseconds. That converted into just over a quarter of a second, which, oddly enough, was roughly equal to the speed of sound. So, it was conceivable that Jack could shoot someone 100 yards away, and they would never hear it coming.

Handguns were not designed to be long-distance tools; that's what rifles are for, but Jack did pretty good nonetheless. He shot 15 times at the steel and hit it all but two shots. Jack had learned that one of the keys to shooting well was to never be satisfied with any given shot. Always strive for perfection, even knowing that perfection is unattainable.

After just an hour of shooting, Jack was exhausted. But it was a contented exhaustion. He put his gear away, reloaded his gun with hollow points and reholstered. He started the SUV and looked down at his cell phone. It still had not rung. He checked for messages, but there were none.

He sighed and looked at the paper sack of pasties that

Florence had given him. He looked out across the gravel pit and reached down to touch the bulk of his gun. Jack had been raised in church, and he knew that those who lived by the sword died by the sword. He thought about it for a moment *Dying by the sword. Was that really such a bad thing?* After all, death was inevitable. It would happen at a time and place of God's choosing. Jack thought about it and suddenly realized that it was important how you lived, but ... it was equally important how you died. And then he thought.

Live with honor ... die with honor.

And then Jack wondered about Amanda, what she might be feeling right now, what she might be thinking, what she might be suffering. Jack was ready to die. He was spiritually fit. But what about Amanda? He hardly knew her. Did she know God? He didn't know ...but he doubted.

And that was all the more reason he needed to save her.

Jack shrugged off the introspection and took out one of Flo's pasties. They were cold now. Made from flour, rutabagas, onions, garlic, salt, pepper and lard ... lots of lard. And then Jack thought *If Bobbie Lee doesn't kill me, these pasties probably will.*

And Jack smiled.

He gobbled down the cold pasty, leaned back in his seat and drifted off to sleep.

Somewhere in Jackpine

THE PINK BATH ROBE LOOKED LONELY DRAPED NEATLY over the chair beside the desk. The chair was a black, imitation leather, cheaply done, and it shone in the dim light of the desk lamp just a few feet away. The bath robe was a fuzzy fleece cloth, the kind that liked to be touched and held against warm skin. But there was no warm skin, not today or the day before. The bath robe hadn't been worn in several days now.

The laptop was open on the desk in front of the chair. It was still plugged in, and every so often the tiny fan would turn on and whir away, doing its only job in the universe: to cool the computer components inside the housing. The curser, like a blinking human eye, like a faithful canine companion, waited at the login prompt, panting patiently, quiescently, secretly wanting to be stimulated by a human host but ... there were no humans to indulge it. So the cursor, and the computer, kept waiting for its master's return.

Suddenly, a sharp thud sounded on the glass window pane over the desk, and the errant bird fell to the ground where it would die of exposure before awakening. But the contents of the tiny office were oblivious to the plight of the bird. Their world was small. Neither the computer, with its cursor, nor the desk or the chair nor the fuzzy, pink bath robe, none of them had any knowledge of the bird's demise. It was just a small sparrow, insignificant as anything in the world, however ... the black, leather book perched quietly beside the computer knew the Truth.

Nothing falls to the earth absent the cognizance of God. Why? Because His eye is on the sparrow. Always ... forever ... unceasing.

CHAPTER 17

PRIOR TO COMING TO JACKPINE, Amanda had been indifferent about duct tape. But now ... she was beginning to develop some very strong opinions, indeed, even emotions about it. Being a city girl, she didn't know that it came in different grades, and strengths, and even a myriad of colors and patterns. And the tape that Bobbie Lee had used to bind her to the chair would not relent. It was thick and strong and heavy. Right about now Amanda felt that duct tape was from the devil.

Amanda had been struggling for over two hours now, trying in vain to loosen or break the tape, but every time she moved, her injured collarbone ached. She decided to rest for a while. She took the time to explore the room around her. It was about 12 feet wide by 16 feet long ... her own, private rectangle of terror. There was a desk in one corner with a laptop open to the login page. What appeared to be a Bible was lying to the left of the computer. A bath robe was draped over the chair. On the wall to her front was a knickknack shelf filled with little glass figurines and tiny statues. One of the knickknacks appeared to be praying hands with the words 'God Answers Prayer.' Once again, Amanda was tempted to pray, to call out to God for help, but ... for some strange reason ... she resisted.

Aside from bedtime prayers as a girl, she hadn't prayed

in her whole life. And those childhood prayers, really hadn't been sincere; they'd been just words or incantations she'd recited by memory, because she'd been told to do it. But now, at this very moment, being duct-taped to a chair by an evil murderer with her certain death imminent, she decided to give prayer a second glance.

There was also a picture of Jesus hanging on the wall beside the shelf, or, at least a person she assumed was Jesus. It was the traditional artist's rendering of the man, and Amanda had seen it in many homes throughout her life ... but ... she'd never really given it much attention. Sure, she'd looked at it, but ... there'd never really been a compelling reason to do more than glance at it in passing.

God answers prayer. Amanda mulled the concept over in her head for a moment. Was it true? Did God really answer prayer? Could He hear her? Was He listening? Amanda didn't know the answers to those questions. However, if God could hear her, then couldn't He also see her? And, if that was true, then why wouldn't He just send someone to rescue her, or, for that matter, save her Himself? She started struggling with her bindings again. Right about now she wasn't feeling very picky about how God saved her, she just wanted the job done.

She wondered again why God would choose to save some and not others. She knew that good things sometimes happened to bad people and that bad, evil things sometimes happened to the most devout people on the planet. She wondered why. And then another thought occurred to her *She'd never in her entire life asked these questions before.* In fact, she'd never asked anything of God, not so much as a Christmas present as a kid or even help on a test in college. Any thoughts of God had been entirely absent from her mind and from her heart until ... and then she thought about Florence Wentley. Florence had prayed for her, not once, but twice, and Amanda couldn't help but hope in her heart that Florence was praying for her again, wherever she was.

And then another thought passed through her mind *If I*

don't believe in God, then why am I thinking about Him so much? Most of her friends either didn't believe in God or didn't care enough to even consider it. Many just didn't have the time of day to deal with it, because they were too busy trying to party and get ahead in their careers.

Amanda looked down at her ankles taped to the chair legs. She struggled again against the sticky plastic, but all it did was hurt her wrists. And then the oddest thought came to her mind. *I'm not busy right now. I have nothing else to do. Maybe I could pray? What would it hurt?* It wouldn't embarrass her because no one would ever know unless she told them, and if she died, well ... same results ... no one would ever know.

Amanda took another look around the room, then back up at the picture of Jesus. And then she thought *Ahh, what the hell! I'll give it a shot.*

And then Amanda prayed.

"Dear God, or Jesus or who ever else you might be called. Please send Jack Ruger to help me."

Monday, 8PM - Somewhere in Jackpine

JACK HAD A FULL TANK OF GAS SO HE DROVE THE BACK roads of Jackpine, hoping for a break. The more he thought about it, the better he felt about using the local militia for this search and rescue operation. He just hoped they didn't do anything stupid or illegal. If they did, the sheriff would never let him live it down.

Most of the roads were pretty clear of snow now, so it was easy driving. The militia was using CB radio channels, so he listened in on their broadcasts just in case they found anything. So far, he was impressed with their organizational skills. They seemed to have a chain of command, and at least some rudimentary discipline among them. Johnny Sterling, who had turned out to be their commanding officer, had called a meeting with his officers and noncoms before making a search pattern for all to follow. They'd started in the southeastern sector of the township, so Jack had gone to the southwest. The basic plan was to drive slowly down the secondary roads, and check the driveway of every summer or vacation home, that is, any property owned by trolls. All those driveways should be plugged with snow; if they weren't, then they were to radio it in before moving in closer. It sounded as good as any other plan, so Jack was doing the same thing.

So far he'd seen nothing out of the ordinary except for one driveway of a homeowner from Chicago. There were fresh tire tracks going into their drive, so Jack had checked it out. It turns out they'd taken the drive up here to do some snow-mobiling over the holidays. After a short conversation, Jack had given them a flyer with Bobbie Lee's picture and warned them not to approach him if they saw him, just phone it in to dispatch. They'd readily agreed and then thanked him for checking on their vacation home.

Jack couldn't help but wonder what was happening to Amanda right now. Was she hurt? Was she being tortured? Was she even still alive? Jack didn't know and couldn't know until he found her. In a way he felt responsible for her plight. If he'd just told her the truth about Sara Sinai, then she would have finished her business here quickly and would already be back home in New York City. But then ... Jack couldn't do that ... for personal reasons.

He shrugged it off and continued driving the roads, searching for anything out of the ordinary. Amanda and Bobbie Lee were out there somewhere, and soon, very soon, one of them would find her. They had to. Or he could never live with himself.

Suddenly, Jack's cell phone started beeping. It was the alarm for the back door of his house that he'd just installed. He quickly found a place to pull over and then logged into his home security system account. First, he pulled up the camera for his back door and the deck. He saw no movement, but the motion sensor lights were on, and he could see tracks in the snow. He moved to the living room camera and that's where he saw a man holding a five-gallon can of gasoline in his left hand. The man was wearing a heavy, winter parka, with a large hood pulled up over his head. The man was turned away, with his back to the camera, but then he looked around and looked straight up into the lens. He took off the hood and smiled at Jack.

Jack threw down the cell phone and slammed the shifter into drive.

Monday, 8:30PM - The House that Jack Built

Bobbie Lee smiled up at the camera and then he laughed out loud. The only sound in the background was the piercing alarm from the glass breakage sensor for the slider off the deck. He set the gas can down and moved over to the fireplace. There were smoldering embers inside, so he moved the glass door to the left. Then he went into the adjacent kitchen and filled a large bucket with water. Bobbie Lee carried it back into the living room and poured it onto the red-hot coals in the fireplace. Hot steam and smoke billowed up and quickly filled the room. The smoke sensors went off a few seconds later, adding to the chaotic sound caused by the glass breakage sensor.

He then poured all the gasoline on Jack's couch, the oak floor and even on the knotty pine walls. He gradually backed out the sliding door and onto the deck. The gas fumes were overpowering him now, and he had to sit down on the deck railing to keep from fainting. It took a few seconds, but the fresh, cold upper peninsula air revived him. Bobby Lee took a few steps back before reaching into his left coat pocket and pulled out the flare gun. It was already loaded, so he simply pointed the gun into the doorway and pressed the trigger. The flare launched immediately and streaked into Jack's house.

The explosion was more than Bobbie Lee had anticipated, and it blew him off the porch and into a snowbank twenty feet away. The wind was blowing around him, and the raging of the fire was making a lot of noise, but his ears were ringing so loud that he heard none of it.

His eyelashes had been completely singed off by the heat, and a sudden throbbing in his head was apparent, but Bobbie Lee appeared not to notice. He was too busy watching the flames lick up the sides of Jack's living room and consume everything it touched.

And then Bobbie Lee did something strange. He reached into his right coat pocket and pulled out a bag of marshmallows, followed by a telescoping metal rod. He pulled the rod out to its full length of three feet and poked a marshmallow onto the end of it. He moved as close to the fire as the heat would allow, and then he calmly roasted his snack. He then popped the hot, sugar treat into his mouth and smiled happily.

Before leaving, Bobbie Lee pulled out his cell phone and then took a short video of Jack's burning home. Then he reversed the camera direction and smiled.

"Merry Christmas, Jack. Do you like the present I gave you? Listen, I'm having a few friends over for dinner tonight, sort of a late, evening repast. Amanda suggested I invite you." and then he paused all the while sneering into the camera. "She's a beautiful woman, Jack, and I don't know how much longer I can control my desires. Better hurry. Oh, and come alone or she dies. This is personal ... between you and me."

He pushed the stop button and then opened a message to Jack's cell number. He attached the video file and then typed in the address and pressed send. He waited patiently for it to load and then go out over the invisible air waves. Once it was done, he placed the cell phone back in his pocket, took one last look at Jack's home as it burned to the ground, and then peacefully walked back into the woods.

WHEN JACK PULLED INTO HIS DRIVEWAY, HE COULD SEE the flames in the sky long before he arrived. He'd already called dispatch and fire trucks were on the way. He could hear their sirens in the distance. Jack came to a stop and jumped out of his SUV. He walked up to the house, but couldn't even get close. The heat was intense and growing by the minute. One quick look told him that the fire department wouldn't be able to save his home. It was done. It was over. It was the house he'd built to share with his beloved, Carrie, the house they were going to have children in and raise a family and slowly grow old in. He'd built it all for her.

Jack watched in shock as the flames rose higher and higher into the night sky. But the fire, as hot as it was, couldn't hold a candle to the rage that Jack was now feeling. And never, in his entire life, had he wanted to kill someone more than he now wanted to kill Bobbie Lee Harper.

One of the fire trucks and several other four-wheel drive vehicles were pulling in now, and the volunteer fire department pressed into service, unrolling hoses and getting ready to fight the fire. But Jack knew it was too late. He ignored the business around him. He was focused on one and only one thing: killing Bobbie Lee.

Just then his phone chimed. He took it out of his coat pocket and opened the message. It took a few seconds to load and play. Jack watched and listened, all the while, anger seethed and bubbled and boiled inside him, like a volcano getting ready to blow. And then he saw the address.

Jack ran past the fire chief who was trying to get his attention, started up his SUV and raced out as quickly as the deep snow and congested driveway would allow.

CHAPTER 18

<u>*Monday, 9PM - Johnny Sterling*</u>

WHEN JOHNNY WAS AT HOME with his kids, he was a good dad. When he was with his wife, he was a good husband. When he was at work, he was the midnight shift supervisor at the plant, and a darn good one at that. But when he donned his uniform and formed up his men, he became a warrior. He became Captain Sterling of the Keweenaw Wildcats.

"Jack's house is burnin' down. The fire department is there, but it looks like a total loss. They're sayin' it was arson."

Captain Sterling released the transmit button on the microphone and moved it away from his mouth. He waited for his lieutenant on the other end to respond before speaking again.

"My guess is it was Bobbie Lee Harper, so that means he's over near Jack's house somewhere, at least for a while until he kin get away. But he's gotta be close. So let's shift half a our men over to that sector. Nobody sleeps till we find this guy."

Johnny was staring over the shoulder of a 16-year-old boy who was looking at a representation of Jackpine township on a Googlemaps app. It was his son, Danny.

"Roger that, Bill. Lemme know when it's done."

He put the microphone back down beside the CB and searched through the computer screen. Florence walked up behind him with a clear, glass carafe of coffee, one in each hand.

"Need more joe?"

Johnny smiled and looked at Florence, holding his heavy glass mug out to her. It was his own private mug with a picture of John Wayne on it. The caption read *A man's gotta do what a man's gotta do.* Johnny had always loved the duke, with his no-nonsense attitude and masculine way of looking at life. It made sense to him, and he'd patterned his life to coincide with the duke's way of thinking. Johnny was a simple man, and he liked things black and white. There were bad guys and there were good guys. Jack Ruger was a good guy, and Bobbie Lee Harper was a bad guy. That's all he needed to know.

It was very clear in his mind now, and he'd communicated his plan to his men. *Kill the bad guy and save the girl.* That was the extent of Johnny Sterling's complexity. It was simple, but when Johnny set his mind to something, nothing could stand in his way, and, if need be, he was willing to kill or die to accomplish the mission.

"Leaded er unleaded, Johnny?"

Captain Sterling laughed out loud. "I think ya already know the answer to that one, Flo."

Florence smiled. "Leaded it is."

Johnny held his cup until she was done pouring. Then he slowly raised it to his lips and blew off the steam. He took a sip and smiled.

"Just the way I like it, Flo. Hot 'nuff ta burn my face off, an black as a cup a tar."

Florence got a concerned look on her face. "So Jack's house is a total loss?"

Johnny nodded. "Fraid so. Nothin' left but hot coals."

Florence frowned. "Jack built that house fer Carrie Parker. They was gonna live there after the marriage."

Johnny tensed his face. "That was the girl who died a cancer a while back?"

Florence nodded and Johnny responded while glancing around the room. "That's really gonna piss 'em off I reckon."

Florence moved to fill more cups. There were about four others in the room, manning radios and maps and computer screens. She called back to him as she filled coffee cups.

"Just find the jerk afore Jack does. The poor man's been through nuff already."

Johnny nodded his head as he responded. "Don't worry, Flo. We'll find the guy, 'n when we do ..." he let the words trail off into a yooper black hole somewhere, and then he turned his head back to Googlemaps.

"What ya findin' son?"

Florence moved back to the kitchen to refill the carafes, but while she was back there, she sat down in a folding chair and bowed her head, placed her elbows on her knees and clasped her hands together in reverence.

"Dear God, Ya gotta help Jack. Keep the boy alive, 'n help 'em find the girl. But don't let the boy die." She paused to wipe a tear away from her eye. Then she bowed down again.

"We need the city girl alive too. She ain't none too smart ... but she's a learnin.' Amen."

And then she stood and went back to work making more coffee. She hated the way the men were always on the move, out doing exciting things, and the women got stuck in support roles, but ... then again ... she wouldn't trade places with Amanda for the world.

Monday, 9:15PM - The Rescue

JACK PARKED HIS SUV OUT AT THE END OF THE DRIVEway. He contemplated calling it in, but thought better of it, remembering Bobbie Lee's words. _Come alone or she dies._

Of course, Jack realized that he might kill her anyway, that, perhaps, she was already dead. But ... that didn't change what he had to do. This was between him and Bobbie Lee Harper. Old scores were always like that.

Jack moved around the back and took out his tactical pack. It had extra flashlights, batteries, knives, nine millimeter mags and AR15 magazines. There was also a water bottle, small first aid kit, some matches, a compass and a poncho.

Jack lifted up the cover to the hidden compartment and pulled out his body armor. He rarely wore it as he just didn't see the need. But ... if ever there was a time for extra protection, it was now. He put it on quickly and fastened the Velcro straps. Then he donned his tactical vest over the top of it, and filled it with extra magazines. Finally, he slipped his arms, one at a time, through the pack straps and hoisted it up to his shoulders.

He then took the AR15 carbine out of the foam cut-outs. It was always battle-ready, set up with an Eotech sight, combination laser sight and flashlight, foregrip with expandable bipod and one-point sling. He wrapped the sling over his shoulder and turned on the Eotech. Then he double-checked to make sure the magazine was loaded and a round was chambered. He tested the laser sight and it was working fine. He hadn't been equipped like this since Afghanistan.

Finally, Jack donned a pair of Generation 3 Mil-Spec night vision goggles. He powered them on and the night suddenly became day. He would go in quietly, without any light, and just maybe he could surprise Bobbie Lee.

Jack closed up his hatch and began moving through the snow with his carbine and pack.

Monday, 9:20PM - The Ambush

Bobbie Lee watched as Jack moved up the driveway toward the house. The drive was a quarter mile long, but there was a full moon tonight and clear skies, so Jack's outline was clear against the brightness of the snow. He was amazed at how boldly Jack moved. Sure, he was stealthy, but ... did he really think that Bobbie Lee would let him sneak up on him like this? If there was one thing he'd learned throughout his years of crime: _the early bird gets the worm._ That's why Bobbie Lee always insisted on calling the shots; he always set up the meeting point, and he was always the first man on the playing field, and the last one to leave when the game was over. That habit alone, had kept him alive on many occasions.

For all those years in prison, Bobble Lee had thought and contemplated what he'd do to Jack when he finally had him. He'd planned it all out in a hundred different ways, fine tuning the plan, then totally changing it, or scrapping the plan altogether and then starting over from scratch. It was his hatred for Jack Ruger that had kept him focused, had given him purpose, had been his sole reason for getting up in the morning, and researching, and staying in shape, and learning so many things about his criminal craft.

There was no denying that Bobbie Lee Harper was a bad guy ... but he was very good at being a very bad guy.

Hatred was power, and he felt it thrumming through his veins now like liquid fire, like electricity in a power line; he just had to focus the energy into something useful and destructive.

And now ... all his hard work was coming to fruition. All he had to do was wait, just a little while longer. Jack Ruger was coming to him, and the excitement was climactic. He watched Jack from the safety of the darkened room and smiled.

Come on Jack. I've been waiting for a very long time. And I herald your coming ... the way the spider greets the fly.

JACK SAW THE BLUE FOUR-WHEEL-DRIVE TRUCK IN THE driveway and grimaced. Bobbie Lee hadn't even bothered to hide it in the garage. He stopped behind an oak tree as he contemplated the last few yards to the house. It was completely dark inside, with not a light for miles around. But Jack's night vision goggles lit up the night, turning it into day for him, but only for him. He was happy to see the darkened house, because that would give him all the advantage he needed.

Jack moved quickly to the edge of the house and up to the small door leading into the garage. He reached out his black, gloved hand and tried the door knob. It turned easily, sending tingles up and down Jack's spine. *I am expected.* But then, what was the surprise in that? He'd been invited. Jack was a very special guest. He opened the door and pushed it open. The garage was empty, save for some garden tools in the corner. A rake, a shovel, a pair of gloves, a small axe and a post-hole digger. Jack hurried inside and closed the door quietly behind him.

And that's when he looked at the door leading into the house and started to doubt his plan. Clearing a house was difficult enough to do with a four-man team, but alone ... it was very dangerous. Jack moved slowly to the door and put his right ear against it to listen. Nothing.

Jack's heart started to race, but he closed his eyes for a moment in an attempt to master his pulse. It was a losing battle. He reached down to touch the knob with his left hand. It opened easily. The door swung inward, and the knob hit the wall to its right, making the loudest sound Jack had ever heard. In reality, it was just a tiny tap, but in the darkness and silence of the house, it seemed like a major explosion. His carbine was up to his shoulder at all times, his eyes darted to the left, then the right, then straight ahead toward the sink. He was in the kitchen. There was an island for food prep in the middle, so he quickly and as quietly as possible moved to ensure there was no one on the other side of it.

It was a modern home, probably not more than five years old with all the features one would expect in a full-time house. Who ever owned this vacation home had money, and lots of it. Jack looked beyond the refrigerator to the living room. He walked slowly, focused on putting one foot in front of the other as quietly as was possible in boots. But every foot fall sounded like a sledge hammer in his ears. And that's when Jack sensed that something was wrong ... out of place. He couldn't put his finger on it, but ... something was either there that shouldn't be there, or was absent and should exist.

He moved to the living room. It was large and open with very few hiding places. And then Jack saw the stairs leading up to the second floor. The floor was carpeted now, so his footsteps were softer. He was grateful for that as he moved to the stairs and began his ascent. And then the uneasy feeling came over him again. *Something is wrong.* He took a few steps up, and the stairs creaked lightly every time he moved.

Jack got halfway up the stairs, and was already peering up, trying to get a view of what lie ahead, when it finally hit him. *This is the quietest house I've ever been in.* There is no noise, save the wind pushing up against the siding. No sound from the refrigerator. No sound of furnace fans kicking in. Inside ,,, it was deathly quiet. *Something is missing?*

And that's when Jack heard a light clank as Bobbie Lee threw the main breaker switch on the electrical panel. Instantly, every light and appliance went on inside the home, and Jack was immediately blinded as the night vision goggles were flooded with way too much light, so much light that it hurt his eyes. He reached up and pulled the goggles off his head and dropped them to the ground. For several seconds he was totally blind, unable to see anything except the bright, whiteness of a million suns. And then the lights went off again, leaving him in darkness. But Jack's eyes couldn't adjust to the sudden change, and he felt as blind and helpless as Hellen Keller at a rock concert.

He didn't hear Bobbie Lee move to the foot of the stairs, but he did hear the click of the Taser as it fired two probes into his body, one in his left butt cheek and the other in the right. It was a perfect shot, and Jack's body stiffened ramrod straight as the voltage traveled back and forth between the two probes. Jack had ridden the lightning during training, but never had he been tased by a man who hated him. Jack went down in a heap and rolled to the bottom of the stairs, hitting his head with a solid crack against the wall. He was out immediately, but that didn't stop Bobbie Lee from pressing the trigger again and again and again. Jack convulsed with every five-second ride, until, finally, one of the probes came loose.

Bobbie Lee walked up to Jack's body and laughed out

loud. Then he reached down with the Taser and drive stunned him a few times, placing the Taser electrodes against Jack's neck and repeatedly pressing the trigger. But Jack's body wasn't feeling it now. He was deep inside a dream, filled with pain and anguish and suffering. But little did he know that the nightmare was just beginning.

Bobbie Lee handcuffed Jack and then drug him up the stairs one at a time, letting Jack's head bounce up and down on the carpeted stairs as he went.

CHAPTER 19

"**J**ACK! WAKE UP! WAKE UP!"
Amanda yelled as loud as she dared, for fear that her captor would come back into the room if he heard her. She yelled over and over again, but Jack Ruger didn't wake up. He lay there on the floor unmoving, silent as a corpse.

"Jack, you have to wake up! Come on, cowboy. Time to saddle up and ride!"Amanda was still duct-taped to the chair in the center of the room. She stopped yelling and looked around her in despair. And then she looked over at the picture of Jesus and sighed out loud.

"I prayed that you'd send Jack Ruger." She paused for a second. "And you did." Her gaze shifted back to Jack's body on the floor just a few feet away. "I guess I should have been more specific."

And then Jack groaned.

"Jack! Good morning, Jack. Time to wake up."

She wanted to kick him in the head, but her feet were securely fastened to the legs of the chair.

"Wakey, wakey, Jack. Time to wake up. Time to kill the bad guy and save the girl."

Jack's head felt like it was filled with compressed air and the air hose was still connected, with the pressure increasing all the while.

"Do you ... have ... any aspirin?"

Amanda smiled softly. *He was alive.*

"They're in my purse, Jack. Will you hand it to me, please?"

Jack smiled despite the intense pain in his head and the rest of his body. He tried to move, but realized his hands were cuffed behind him, and that his legs were duct-taped at the knees and also at the ankles. He suddenly felt very helpless.

"Amanda."

"Yes, Jack."

"Life is tough."

Part of Amanda wanted to hug him, while another part of her wanted to kill him.

"Yes, Jack. I know."

"Life is tough. But it's a lot tougher when you're stupid."

Amanda cocked her head to one side in disbelief. "Are you calling me, stupid, Jack?"

Jack chuckled softly to himself. "Do you know who said that, Amanda?"

She thought for a moment."No, but it does make sense. Are you a philosopher now, Jack?"

"It was John Wayne. The Duke said that."

Jack lifted his head as far as he could and turned toward Amanda. She gasped when she saw the bruises, cuts and blood on his face where Bobbie Lee had punched and kicked him repeatedly.

"Jack, you look terrible. Are you okay?"

"I'm going to kill Bobbie Lee Parker."

Amanda's head sagged down onto her chest.

"That's nice."

"Have you ever been tased in the butt, Amanda?"

Amanda couldn't help but smile.

"No, Jack. I haven't."

Jack looked up at her again. Blood dripped down into his eyes as he spoke. "It's a real pain in the ...." He winced in anguish and couldn't finish the sentence.

Amanda sucked in a deep breath, and then let it out slowly again. "Jack, are you going to rescue me or just lie there on the floor bleeding?" She didn't give Jack time to answer. "And that's another thing, Jack. Why did you ask me out to dinner and then change your mind about it?" She waited for an answer, but none came to her. "You can't do that, Jack. You have to take me out to dinner. You gave me your word, and now I'm holding you to it. So get off your lazy butt and let's get out of here."

Jack didn't move.

"Jack?"

There was no sound from the body on the floor.

"Jack? I'm hungry. Let's go."

But Jack just lay there, drifting in and out of consciousness. And then Amanda heard the faint whirring of the garage door opener, then a car engine as it pulled in. Bobbie Lee Harper had returned.

She looked down at Jack, who was motionless and bleeding on the carpet. Then she looked up on the wall and saw a shiny, purple, glass figurine of a unicorn on the shelf. She didn't believe in unicorns anymore. And then she looked at Jesus. He was still there, looking at her, almost smiling.

Amanda hung her head a moment and sighed. Then she looked back up at him.

"Okay, Jesus. I asked for Jack and I got Jack. Will you please send some more help ... someone who isn't beaten to a pulp, someone who can save us. I'm not picky here. Just send anybody you want. Man, woman, child. I don't care. Just get us out of this mess, please."

And then Amanda closed her eyes and thought about it. Suddenly, from out of nowhere an old adage came to her. *There are no atheists in foxholes.* And she knew in her heart that it was true. Because, for the first time in her life, she was praying. And ... she was meaning it.

BOBBIE LEE WALKED INTO THE ROOM AND CLOSED THE door behind him. He was still wearing his coat. It was black wool and came down to the middle of his thighs.

"He still out?"

Amanda glared over at the man. "Well, in his defense, you did tase him and then beat him near to death."

Bobbie Lee shrugged. "I thought he was tougher than that. I guess not."

Amanda didn't say anything.

"Ya know, Amanda ... may I call you Amanda?"

Again, she didn't answer.

"I rotted in that prison cell for over four years."

He made eye contact with her.

"Four years, Amanda! I can see that you're sympathizing with me about it and I appreciate that."

He walked over to the chair beside the desk. He tossed the bath robe onto the floor and moved the desk chair around so it was facing Amanda.

"I suspect that I thought about it so much that I built Jack up into some kind of undefeatable monster or something. Like he was this big hero; this giant that couldn't be slain."

He sat down in the desk chair facing her. Then he crossed his left leg over his right and crossed his arms over his chest.

"But ya know what, Amanda?" He looked down at the mass of flesh on the floor. "I just slew the giant, and he wasn't all that tough. I was smarter than him. I'm stronger and I'm faster."

He moved his right hand up and pointed down at Jack. "You see how tough he is, Amanda?"

He grunted softly. "He was very disappointing, Amanda. Very disappointing. I was hoping for more, but ... anticlimactic at best."

Bobbie Lee stood up and kicked Jack on the back as hard as he could over and over again.

"You let me down, Jack! You let me down!" And then his kicks lessened in number and severity, but didn't quite stop."I

138

had you built up into ... " He paused as if searching for the perfect words. "This indefatigable, indomitable, resilient man that couldn't be beaten! But you let me defeat you so quickly and so easily! That makes me mad, Jack! That makes me angry!"

He cocked his foot and kicked Jack one last time before sitting back down again. And then he looked over at Amanda, his steel, green eyes searching her as if measuring her mettle. And when he finally spoke, it was more a guttural spewing than a sentence.

"Are you going to disappoint me too, Amanda? Are you going to let me down?"

Amanda shook her head as best she could from side to side. "No, Bobbie Lee. Of course not. I won't let you down."

Bobbie Lee got back up out of his chair and stepped over to her. He grabbed her face with his left hand and squeezed as hard as he could. Her cheeks pressed together and she screamed.

He bent down and pressed his lips against her own. Amanda tried to respond, tried to give him what he wanted just so he wouldn't kill her, but ... she couldn't. And then she realized *I would rather die.* But she said nothing aloud. Bobbie Lee kept talking.

"When I get disappointed ... I get angry."

Bobbie Lee shook his head slowly from side to side. "Don't make me angry. I don't like being angry."

Amanda looked down at Jack. He still wasn't moving, but she saw the slight rising and falling of his chest as he lay on the floor below her. She didn't say anything for fear of saying the wrong thing and being beaten for it.

"Jack let me down, but I know that you won't." He nudged Jack in the back without kicking him. "Him ... I thought he was the main course. But ... now ... I realize that he was just an appetizer, the pregame show, the warm up."

Amanda looked away over at the picture of Jesus on the wall, trying to draw some hope or courage or confidence, but none was immediately forthcoming.

"Don't look away from me, Amanda! Don't disappoint me!" He moved his face down close to her own and stared straight into her eyes. "Don't you understand, Amanda?"

And then he kissed her again. She tried to respond. He backed his face away from her. "You are my last hope. You are my love ... my chosen love." He closed his eyes and sighed as if discouraged. "Jack ..." He motioned to the floor with a wave of his head. "Jack is just a warm up, the foreplay. You Amanda ... you are the main event!"

And then he turned and left the room.

CHAPTER 20

Tuesday, 1AM - Looking for Jack

BOBBIE JOE NAPIER WAS A SIMPLE man. He didn't have big thoughts, not many dreams, he just wanted to get up in the morning, go to the machine shop and put in his eight hours. Then he'd come home and watch some TV and eat a microwave dinner. He especially liked the macaroni and cheese with chicken thighs. And tator tots. Bobbie Joe Napier just loved tator tots.

Some people would say that Bobbie Joe's life was dull and boring, but ... it was the life he'd chosen and the life he loved. He'd been single his whole life, and he liked it that way. He never got lonely. Well ... almost never. But on those few occasions when he did feel lonely, on those long, hard, cold nights in the yoo pee winters, Bobbie Joe just looked around him at the cluttered mobile home and sighed with contentment. There were three gun safes to his left, twenty thousand rounds of ammo to his right, and a yellow Gadsden flag on the wall in front of him with a coiled snake that said "Don't tread on me." And to top it all off ... he had a pole barn. Bobbie Joe Napier was living the American dream.

He throttled up his snowmobile as he left Jackpine for the second time that night. Florence had left the diner open all night to act as the militia's headquarters during the search and rescue operation for Amanda Walker. But now ... Jack was missing as well, so the search had been expanded.

Bobbie Joe had joined the local militia about ten years ago as soon as it had been formed, and he'd never regretted it. Most people from downstate thought of the militia as a paramilitary organization that wanted a violent overthrow of the government. But Bobbie Joe didn't see it that way. He got free firearms training and lots of opportunities to shoot expensive guns. It was a lot of fun.

His favorite hobby was long-distance shooting, and he was one of the designated snipers for the Keweenaw Wildcats. That's what Johnny Sterling had named their unit, and no one had complained. It was pretty cool. His caliber of choice was three oh eight, but he could make a decent head shot at five hundred yards with five five six rounds as well. It was a satisfying challenge with a very practical use, which he exploited every November during deer season to fill his freezer with meat.

And so ... when the Wildcats had been called up, he'd drug his sorry butt off the couch and gassed up his snow buggy for the big adventure.

But little did Bobbie Joe know, this would be the adventure of a lifetime.

Tuesday, 1:30AM, Jack and Amanda

"Jack? Are you awake yet?"

Amanda's hands were numb now from the duct tape, so she moved them again to get the blood flowing back into them. The pain in her collarbone had long subsided, overwhelmed by a host of other aches and pains. She could only imagine what Jack must be feeling right now after being beaten so severely by Bobbie Lee Harper.

"Are you awake, Jack?" A part of her wanted to let him sleep, but she knew in her heart that if he didn't awaken, they would likely die at the hands of Bobbie Lee Harper. There only chance was to escape, and she didn't know how to do it on her own. Oddly enough, life at a New York City publishing company hadn't prepared her for this.

"Jack, I'm having trouble sleeping, and I was hoping you could sing to me."

And then she heard Jack laugh softly, barely a whisper. She smiled. "You're awake, aren't you."

Jack's pain-wracked body sighed out loud. "Well, Amanda, it's pretty hard to sleep with you talking to me all time."

Amanda looked over at the picture of Jesus again, then glanced down at Jack on the floor. "I knew you would come to save me."

Jack tried to laugh, but the pain in his ribs wouldn't let him. Some of them had to be broken with the beating he'd taken. "Amanda, we need to talk, and I think this might be our last chance."

"Don't talk like that, Jack. I prayed that God would send you and He did. So now you have to save us. So figure something out."

Jack let out his breath and then slowly took it back in again. Even under ideal circumstances, this would be a difficult conversation, but now ... they would probably both be dead in the morning, and ... it was now or never.

"You don't have to take me out to dinner if you don't want to, Jack. Florence told me about your history, what with Carrie and all that's happened to you." And then she closed her eyes and thought about what it might have felt like to endure the death of all those loved ones.

"It's not that, Amanda." He hesitated and that got Amanda's attention even more.

"Well, what it is it then?"

There was silence in the room. Jack listened to the howling of the wind outside the window.

"I haven't been totally honest with you, Amanda." He tried to open his eyes, but fluid had dried and caked them both shut. Amanda didn't say anything.

"You've been looking for Sara Sinai, and I know who she

is."

That's when Amanda remembered their first conversation in his office and that tiny glint of doubt she'd felt when she'd first asked him about Sara Sinai.

"Talk to me, Jack. Who is she?"

Jack tried to move his body around to face her, even though he couldn't see. After several seconds of excruciating pain, he gave up and just lie still.

"Amanda, have you ever been in a situation where the answer to a question was right there in front of you, but you couldn't see it?"

Amanda nodded, but Jack couldn't see it.

"It's like that with Sara Sinai. She's been hiding in plain sight the whole time you've been in Jackpine."

And then it dawned on Amanda.

"Is it Florence. Is she Sara Sinai?"

Jack almost laughed, but stifled it to avoid the pain penalty. "No, Amanda. It's not Flo."

And then he was silent. If Amanda hadn't been duct-taped to the back of her chair, she would have been on the edge of it. She had no choice but to wait patiently. And, when Jack finally spoke, Amanda's heart beat wildly in her chest.

"It's me, Amanda. I am Sara Sinai."

Tuesday, 1:45AM, On the Hunt

Bobby Joe Napier was exhausted, but the freezing cold wind helped to keep him awake. He was pulled over now at the side of the road and standing inside the boughs of a big Jack Pine tree, taking cover from the wind. He pulled his goggles onto the top of his head to take a better look around, then he opened up the waxed paper and looked down at the chicken pasty. He'd kept it inside his snowmobile suit to keep it from freezing.

He raised it up to his mouth and bit off a big chunk and savored it for a moment as he chewed. He loved pasties, and

144

he'd eat them everyday if he could. And then he thought for a moment about what he'd just said. *I do eat them everyday.*

Bobbie Joe had been down every back road in his sector that he knew of at least. He thought hard. *Where have I not looked?* He quickly finished gobbling down the last of his pasty, then he pulled a bottle out of his shirt pocket from the inside of his snow suit. He uncapped the bottle and took a big pull, letting the red-hot liquid burn his throat all the way down to his gullet. Pasties 'n Jack Daniels. There wasn't a better meal anywhere as far as he was concerned.

He capped the bottle back up and returned it to his inside pocket before zipping the snow suit back up. Bobbie Joe looked out into the night, and it was as black as far as the eye could see. Nothing but blowing snow out there and darkness. And then, as if on cue, the wind stopped. A few seconds later the snow settled down, and Bobbie's visibility got a whole lot better. Bobbie Joe looked up into the sky and could see nothing but clouds, but ... he thought they were starting to clear up a bit now.

He looked to the east. There, on the horizon. *Was that a light?* Bobbie Joe squinted his brow and shielded his eyes with his hand for a moment. He walked back over to his snow machine and dug his binoculars out of his back pack. He raised them up to his eyes and peered out into the darkness.

When he brought the optics down from his face, he whispered out to the void in down-home, yooper dialect.

"Holy shit 'n shinola!"

And then he fired up his machine and raced off into the night.

Tuesday, 1:45AM, Jack and Amanda

AMANDA SHOOK HER HEAD BACK AND FORTH IN DENIAL. "That's not possible, Jack. You can't be Sara Sinai."

Jack didn't want to argue with her about it, but he knew that this had to be cleared up before Bobbie Lee came back.

So he just cut to the chase.

"Carrie was my fiance, the love of my life. She'd always wanted to be a writer, and I always encouraged her to follow her dream. She was working on her first novel when she was diagnosed with ovarian cancer."

Jack was silent a moment, as if collecting the strength to continue on. "Even after she was in hospice, she just kept working on it. She wanted so much to finish it before she died. Then at the end, when she no longer had the strength to continue on her own, she would dictate to me and I would type it into the computer as she talked."

Amanda suddenly squirmed in the chair as much as her bonds would allow. She all of a sudden felt like she was intruding on holy ground, like she was trespassing somewhere she had no business. But she remained silent.

"I remember the day she finally realized that we weren't going to finish it in time. I was feeding her ice chips, because that's all she could keep down anymore. She was so weak, and by then she could hardly talk. All I could do was cry. I tried not to, but ... I just couldn't hold it back anymore. The whole time I'd been telling her that she was going to pull through, that God would heal her. It would be a miracle, and that she would get back on her feet and write a million novels, that we would have kids and a long life together. But ... I think I was telling her that mostly to convince myself of that, because I just couldn't face up to the reality of life without her. I loved her so much. I still do."

Amanda started to cry, but she tried not to make a sound, so Jack would finish speaking.

"In the end ... she was ready to die. The pain was so great that she was on morphine almost nonstop. Most of the time I just sat by her bed and held her hand."

Jack hesitated for a few seconds. The wind outside appeared to let up. "And then ... I kissed her on the forehead, she told me she loved me, and then she died."

But Amanda could no longer hold it in. She started to cry

out loud. "I'm ... sorry, Jack. I'm so sorry."

Jack smiled sadly. "I know. Me too."

And then neither of them said a word for fifteen minutes. Jack didn't cry. He had cried himself out months ago. Amanda's whimpers and sniffles filled the room, but ... they eventually died down to nothing as she sat there grim, lost in her mixed emotions of grief for Jack and his loss, then to the surety of her own death at the hands of a homicidal maniac.

Jack's voice broke the stillness. "After Carrie died I waited a few months. I was lost in my own sadness. I wasn't much of a cop then. Thank God there's very little crime in Jackpine. The people knew what was happening to me, but they didn't talk about it much and neither did I. But I knew they cared about me. Flo was like a sister and a mom all rolled into one. We managed to talk about it one night and that made me feel better. I was losing too much weight and that's when she started to cook all my meals for me. Sometimes she'd even drop them off at the house or the office, if I didn't stop by to pick up the food. I always felt guilty about putting her out of her way when she did that, so I made sure to stop off at the diner to get my meals so it would be easier for her. I forced myself to eat. And then ..."

Jack stopped talking, as if thinking back in time and reliving the past. "And then I got this idea to finish Carrie's book for her, so I started writing. It wasn't as hard as I thought it was going to be, because we'd been such a team the whole way. I've always been a fairly good writer, and I knew Carrie's style and ... the inside of her heart. And the weirdest thing happened. When I started writing her stories ... I felt like she was there beside me, encouraging me, asking me to keep going."

Jack realized he'd been holding his head up off the floor for the past few minutes, He let it drop down onto the carpet again before going on. "And so I finished the first novel, and that helped me say good bye to her. And then ... one day, when I was going through some of her things, I ran across this notebook and she had the outlines to three more stories in there. And the stories were good."

The publishing part of Amanda had started to kick in, and she was so fascinated at his story, that she said nothing to interrupt him.

"I started in on the second novel, and at first I couldn't do it without her. But then ... I tried something really strange. When I wrote, I would use her laptop, and I would put her stuffed animals up on the desk beside me. She had this one unicorn, a white one with a pink horn. She loved it and it was beside her the day she died. It helped me to write. And then one day I put on her bath robe. It didn't fit me at all, but ... it had just been laying there on the carpet since the hospital. And ... I don't know if it was just my imagination, but ... I could smell her skin and her hair on the collar. And it made me feel closer to her. It inspired me. And, it was almost like I was with her again." Jack paused. "Does that sound too weird? Dressing up in a woman's clothes?"

The tears had dried on Amanda's cheeks, making her skin feel tight. "No. I don't think so. In fact, I think that's the most romantic thing I've ever heard."

"I just finished writing the last of Carrie's stories just a few days ago. And it's really weird, but ... I miss writing now."

Amanda smiled softly. "Maybe you're a writer, Jack. Maybe it's a part of you now."

"I suppose that's possible. But ... I have no more stories left to write."

Amanda was silent for a moment. "I find that hard to believe. I bet you have a lot of stories inside you. Stories about Jackpine and all the things that have happened to you. You've had a painful life, Jack, but ... it certainly hasn't been boring."

Jack didn't answer her. "Jack, are you there? Maybe you could write a detective or a cop novel. You'd be good at that, and the genre sells well."

Jack thought about it for a few seconds. "I don't know, Amanda. It was different before. I started writing for Carrie, then I wrote for myself to help me through all the sadness, but now ... I don't know. I don't have to write to exist anymore."

And then a thought occurred to Amanda. "Jack, you made a lot of money off those first three books. Don't you want to make more?"

Jack tried to smile, but a sudden pain shot through his back. He winced out loud, but quickly suppressed it. "Yeah. I was surprised at how well they sold. I did make a lot of money, but that's not why I did it. I don't need any more money. I live a pretty simple life." He paused. "I like my life simple. I gave most of the money to the American Cancer Society."

Amanda listened in near disbelief. "I've never met a man like you, Jack." And that's when she understood what real love is, that love was possible, that there really were good men out there who thought more about others than their own selfish desires. And ... it made her hope.

"Jack, I wish I could have a man like you someday."

She waited for his response, wanting it to be positive, wanting it to hold a future, but she was disappointed.

"Amanda I have to be honest with you. I'm broken inside. I don't work right anymore. I've never told anyone this but ... there are some days I'm quite comfortable with the idea of my own death. In fact, right now death sounds pretty good to me. I'd get to see Carrie again ..."

He let the words trail off. Amanda's heart sank.

"But ... I can't let myself die right now. There are people who need me. And ... if Bobbie Lee kills me, then ... he's going to kill others. You, maybe Flo or a dozen other people we don't even know about. A man like him doesn't stop killing, and I know firsthand the pain he leaves in his wake is unbearable to a lot of people."

And it was at that moment in time, that precise second, when Jack decided to live for one more day, just long enough to kill Bobbie Lee Harper, just long enough to save the girl, just long enough to suffer more pain and sorrow and altruism. Yes, he would live until tomorrow. Then ... he would do his

Jackpine Strong

best to kill Bobbie Lee, to stop his unbridled killing spree.

And the day after tomorrow ... who knows. For Jack, he pretty much took each day as it came up. One day at a time, that's all he ever promised himself. But first ... he had to live that one more day or else tomorrow would never come.

Amanda remained strangely quiet. She was suddenly in love with a man with very little will to live. She was tied to a chair, awaiting her imminent torture and death. The picture on the wall beckoned to her again and she looked over to it.

Jack couldn't save her but ... was there still hope?

CHAPTER 21

<u>*Tuesday, 5AM - Listening Post*</u>

BOBBY JOE NAPIER LOOKED OUT AT the front yard from high atop a pine tree two hundred yards away. He'd been watching the house for almost two hours now, and hadn't seen anyone for over an hour. Initially, he'd watched as Bobbie Lee Harper had driven Jack's patrol SUV into the garage and shut the door. There was a blue pick-up truck with a nice cap on the back in front of the garage door right now. Bobby Joe had always wanted a truck like that, and he contemplated the idea in his mind right now. Perhaps he would buy one if his raise came through as scheduled. Or maybe not.

Right now there was only one light on in the house, and that was on the second floor. The curtains were drawn, but in the dead of night in the yoo pee, that light had carried a long, long way. And that's how he'd found the house. He hadn't approached the house at all, had just called it in on his radio and waited for instructions. Captain Sterling had been away from the radio, and hadn't returned the transmission for a full half hour. Bobbie Joe had given him the location and a full situation report. The captain had ordered him to set up a listening post and to observe and report. He would organize the rescue force and plan of attack. They would be there within the hour. That had been over an hour ago, and Bobbie Joe was starting to get concerned.

What would he do if the bad guy tried to leave. Should he just shoot him outright and let the cops sort it out? He tried to remember what Jack had said about use of deadly force, but ... Bobbie Joe was a simple man, not into book learning or laws, so he just lived through his life doing what made good sense to him. That had worked for him so far, and he reckoned he'd just keep on doing it until it stopped working for him.

His three oh eight rifle was hanging by the sling on a branch that he'd sawed off. He looked at the open end of the branch and saw a little sap oozing out. He liked the smell of pine sap, but hated when it got on his clothes or his skin. It seemed to stick there forever, with a vehemence that outlived Methuselah. And that's when he'd gotten the hankering for a hot cup of pine needle tea.

He'd broken off several of the pine boughs and placed them atop two other stronger branches forming a bench seat. He'd already tied himself to the trunk using a rachet strap, just in case the seat broke. He was a good thirty feet off the ground with a clear view to the house, so he if he fell it would likely be a life-ending or life-changing event. But, at least for now, he was comfortable and warm as the pine boughs did a great job of blocking the wind.

His pack was hanging eighteen inches away, so he reached over and dug through it until he came out with an MRE pouch. He pulled out the flameless ration heater bag and replaced the MRE. He took his tin cup and filled it with snow and then shoved in about twenty pine needles. Bobbie Joe took out his canteen and noticed how light it felt. Not much water left and it was best not to waste it on heating tea. He thought about the whiskey in his flask of his shirt pocket, wondering if that would work to activate the chemical heater, but quickly disregarded that idea. The whiskey was certainly more precious to him than mere water. Besides, he knew that the ration heater contained finely powdered magnesium metal, and it was mixed with a small amount of iron, and table salt. To activate the reaction, a small amount of water had to be added. The boiling point of water would quickly be reached as the chemical reaction occurred, but, quite frankly, Bobbie Joe didn't know a lot about chemistry. Would it work with whiskey? He didn't know. For all he knew it would create an unstable chemical reaction and blow up in his lap. He didn't need that.

However, from experience he knew of a simple workaround. His bladder was already full to bursting, so he stood on two branches while undoing his zipper. The rest of the operation was simple mechanics as he urinated, being careful to save just enough to activate the chemical ration heater.

He loved those ration heaters. In this kind of weather, it would do double duty: it would heat his tea and also warm up his hands and his lap, provided he situated it carefully and didn't spill it.

Ten minutes later, Bobbie Joe was warming his insides, sipping the pine tea, feeling the warmth of it go down into his stomach. He drank this tea almost everyday. It was free, full of vitamin C, and didn't taste all that bad once you got used to it. He surmised to himself; there were a lot of things in life that took some getting used to.

It was still dark, so after finishing his tea, Bobbie Joe tried to contact the captain again. He needed to know what the hold-up was and what he should do until they reached him. Bobbie Joe watched the house carefully as he spoke softly into the radio. A few minutes later he breathed a sigh of relief and put the radio back in his pack. They were en route. The calvary was coming!

Tuesday, 6AM - Breaking Dawn

IN HER DREAM, AMANDA SMELLED BACON, AND IT MADE her mouth water. And that was odd, because she rarely ate bacon or meat of any kind. She remembered Flo's omelette, the one that had sent her to the hospital just a short while ago. It seemed like a lifetime away, but ... so much had happened in so short a time.

The dream seemed so real to her, like she really could smell the bacon, but her body was wracked with too much pain to have an appetite. She slowly came back into the real world, and sniffed the air.

The bacon was real.

She looked down at the floor, expecting to see Jack lying there, but ... he was gone. Immediately, she panicked. A host of questions flooded into her brain. *Where did he go? Was he dead? Had he escaped and left her to die?* She didn't know the answer to any of these questions, and it drove her crazy to guess.

Once more, as she'd done a hundred times since being bound to the chair, Amanda looked back over at the picture of Jesus. He was still there, just looking at her, saying nothing, doing nothing, but ... at least He was still there; that's more than she could say for Jack Ruger.

She sighed. That was probably a bit too harsh. For all she knew Jack was dead, and, in his defense, he had come here to rescue her at risk of his own life. But then she reasoned, *Well, it is his job. He is a cop.* And that thought was quickly followed by this one: *Jack came to save me, and, because of it, he's going to die.*

And then ... the most unusual thought came to her mind. *Why don't you save yourself?* She pondered it in her mind, mulled it over, chewed on it a while, looked for flaws, for lack of logic, common sense, practicality. In the end she decided she had nothing to lose. If she did nothing ... she would die. And, as a bonus, if she did manage to get away, then she could help Jack as well. Yes, that just might be crazy enough to work.

And then she focused on the room around her, on her bonds, and her assets and liabilities, and, slowly, over time, a plan began to form.

Tuesday, 6:15AM - The Last Supper

"I suppose you know I'm going to kill you today, Jack."

Jack didn't answer. His eyes were swollen completely shut from the beating last night, and he was in total darkness.

"Why haven't you eaten any of your food?"

Jack still didn't answer. He smelled the food, but he just wasn't hungry. Besides, he couldn't see it, and he didn't want to give Bobbie Lee the satisfaction of watching him fumble around blind at the table.

"Ya know, Jack, you don't have to be a poor sport about all this." Bobbie Lee was sitting at the table about three feet away from Jack. "It's not my fault you came looking for me. You could have let the girl die. You could have gotten into your SUV and drove away forever, and I probably would never have been able to find you."

Bobbie Lee looked down at the nine millimeter Glock beside his plate of bacon and eggs. "But no! You had to be the hero. You had to rescue the girl, kill the bad guy and go down in history as a famous law man."

He reached his right hand up and placed it on the grip of the Glock. "I could kill you right now, Jack. I could. It would be so easy. My hand is on the gun right now. You're blind. You can't stop me. You, Jack Ruger, the man who hunted me down, shot me, and put me behind bars, is now my prisoner."

Bobbie Lee raised the pistol and hefted it in his hand. "Don't you see the irony in that, Jack?" Bobbie Lee looked up at the ceiling and smiled. "I love irony. It's so, how shall we say it ... ironic?" And then he laughed again.

He put the pistol back down on the table to the right of his plate and picked up his fork. He shoveled several spoonfuls of scrambled eggs into his mouth and chewed hungrily. He paused long enough to take a drink of orange juice.

"Now Jack, you're not eating. I went to a great deal of trouble to fix this for you, so the least you can do is find enough courtesy in your heart to eat it."

Bobbie Lee set down his fork. His face grew stern.

"This is the last meal you'll ever eat, my friend. Because I'm going to kill you as soon as the sun comes up."

Inside Jack, a part of him felt relieved, but ... then he thought of Amanda. She was still tied up in the bedroom upstairs. If he died ...

"What are you going to do with Amanda?"

A smile magically appeared on Bobbie Lee's face. He propped both elbows up on the table to either side of his plate and leaned forward, just a bit. "Why, I'm going to kill her, Jack, but ... you certainly must have figured that out by now."

Jack tried to slow his breathing. "Yes, I know that, Bobbie Lee, but ... what are you going to do to her before that?"

Bobbie Lee leaned back before speaking. The wooden chair creaked just a bit. "I'm going to pleasure her, Jack. I'm going to make love to her over and over and over again. After all, it's the least I can do to her for a sacrifice of this magnitude."

He relaxed his posture and picked up a piece of extra crisp bacon in his left hand and popped it into his mouth. Jack could hear the crunching as the bacon ground back and forth against the man's teeth. Jack wanted to kill him, wanted to rip out those teeth chewing the bacon, and that's all he could think of doing at the moment. His emotions were so intense, that it clouded his thinking. Jack breathed slowly and deeply, lowering his heart rate, trying to center himself and find the focus of his situation.

He was blind, helpless. No, not helpless. Blind. There was a difference. Jack could hear the grating of the man's teeth. He guessed him to be three feet away, directly across from him. He knew Bobbie Lee was right handed, so he suspected the pistol was to the right of Bobby Lee, lying on the table beside his plate. He would wait for the right moment.

"If you could just give me a warm, wet washcloth, then maybe I could moisten my eyes enough to open them up and see to eat?"

Bobbie Lee's laughter rang out, echoed across the room, and crescendoed as it continued. It lasted a full ten seconds, but Jack didn't move, he simply waited until the laughter died down.

"Oh, Jack. That is so funny. You are appealing to my better nature, when you perfectly well know that I have none."

Jack feigned laughter. "Well, you must know that I had to try, Bobbie Lee. You can't very well expect me to give up without a fight, now can you?"

Bobbie Lee smiled. "Now that's the Jack Ruger I've grown to know and hate. That's the spirit, Jack! Never give up! After all, you're the good guy, and everyone knows the good guys always win, right?"

Jack's face hardened. "Fred Wentley was the good guy, and he didn't win."

The smile on Bobbie Lee's face slowly changed into a frown, like soft plastic being heated over a register grate. "That's true, Jack. And I think you've just stumbled over one of the most important principles in life. A little late perhaps, but ... nonetheless, you've figured it out."

He picked up his fork again and held it there in front of him. "The bad guys almost always win, Jack. It's always been that way, from time immemorial. I mean, think about it. I shot Fred and his wife and they both died. You eventually did catch me and bring me back to face so-called justice, but ... think about it, Jack. How many crimes did I commit that will never be paid for? How many people have I killed? How many women have I raped? How many have I maimed? I don't expect you to know the answer to that, because, quite frankly, I don't know the answer myself. I didn't keep track. We're talking thousands, Jack. Maybe tens of thousands of crimes that I'll never have to pay for. Isn't it great!"

Jack lowered his head. "I guess that depends on your perspective."

Bobbie Lee nodded his head slowly. And then the smile

returned to his face. "Now, Jack, you're going to find that many of the truths we cling to depend greatly on our own point of view." And then he laughed again. "Do you recognize that line, Jack? It's a quote from Obe-wan Kenobe in *Star Wars*. Man I just love that show. It's a shame that Darth Vader guy turned back to the light just before he died." And then he looked off into the darkness. "That was so disappointing. At least for me personally, I mean."

Jack said nothing more. He just listened intently to every sound that Bobbie Lee made. And when he heard the sound of a metal fork scraping across a glass plate, Jack pushed the heavy, wooden table forward as fast as he could and into Bobbie Lee's lower rib cage. It happened so fast, that Bobbie Lee had no time to react. The Glock pistol skittered quickly off the table and onto the floor several feet away.

Jack continued pushing the table forward, warding off the pain that it caused his ribs and shoulders until he felt Bobbie Lee's legs tangled up in his own. Then, he dropped all his weight down onto the man's groin. Bobbie Lee grunted as Jack's knees drove down into him, knocking the wind out of his lungs. Jack's heart filled with glee when he heard it. And then he started to raise his fist over his face and drive them down into the man's head over and over again. He felt Bobbie Lee's cheekbones crack and splinter, and then his jawbone as well.

But then Jack's left fist met nothing but ceramic tile as Bobbie Lee moved his head to one side. The bones in Jack's hand broke, taking out some of his aggression and steam. Then he felt his body being shoved to the left as Bobbie Lee hooked his right leg over Jack's throat and pushed him onto his back.

Suddenly, without warning, Bobbie Lee was on top of Jack and pummeling him mercilessly. Jack tried to block the blows but couldn't. In desperation and rage, he roared as loud as he could and reached up with both hands, even the broken one and grabbed onto both sides of Bobbie Lee's head. Jack arched his head up as he pulled Bobbie Lee's face down toward him closing the gap. He jammed both thumbs into Bobbie Lee's eyes and began to wiggle them around as violently as he could. Bobbie Lee shrieked in pain like a wild animal. Jack reached up with his mouth as far as he could and bit into his nose. He tasted the coppery flow of blood as it seeped down into his open mouth.

Without warning, Bobbie Lee pushed back as hard as he could, wresting himself from Jack's grasp. Jack tried to follow him, but his blindness prevented it. He halted his movement, waiting, listening. Then he heard the gunshot and felt the round fly passed his head. Jack froze in place.

"If you move ... I'll kill you."

The pain in Jack's rib cage and shoulders and face returned with a vengeance, heightened by the realization that his gamble hadn't paid off. Bobbie Lee had found the gun and it was pointed straight at Jack's head. He decided not to move.

"Did you expect me not to put up a fight, Bobbie Lee? You know better than that. That's not who I am."

Bobbie Lee smiled again. Blood was running down both eyes and onto his cheeks. There were teeth marks on both sides of his nose that would result in a permanent scar. Jack's only regret was that he couldn't see it for himself, but he knew that he must have hurt him.

"Yes, I see that. I underestimated you." He slid himself back against the wall and used it to support himself as he stood to his feet and struggled to catch his breath. "I won't let that happen again. I assure you."

Bobbie Lee blinked his eyes several times to get the blood away from the center so he could see better. Everything was fuzzy, and his eyes felt like sticks had been jammed into them. The left eye appeared to be worse than the right, and that thought relieved him, as he was right-eye dominant with a firearm. He would definitely need medical attention when all this was over. His cheeks were already beginning to fill with fluid as they swelled and puffed up.

But for now, he looked down at Jack, who had rolled over onto his back and was breathing heavily. Bobbie Lee smiled. "That was fun, Jack. Got my heart pumping." And then he waited for a response but none came. "Maybe you're not such a disappointment after all."

Jack did his best to slow his breathing, but he was having trouble. The latest fight had damaged his ribs even further.

"I realize that the smart and safest play is to just shoot you right now. Then go upstairs, rape the woman, shoot her and then be on my way to a new life. But ... I just can't bring myself to do that. Do you realize how long I've planned this thing out? How hard I've worked to pull this meeting off?"

And then he took a few steps backward to stand beside the sink. He jammed the pistol inside his belt in the small of his back. Then he turned on the water and soaked the wash cloth before raising it up to his face and cleaning away the blood. He was surprised by the volume of blood that had collected on the cloth. It hurt when he smiled but that didn't stop him from laughing out loud.

And then he turned away from the sink and looked at Jack lying on the floor.

"I'm honored to have you as my former nemesis."

He dabbed the cloth against his left cheek. "I challenge you, Jack. To pistols at dawn!"

And then he turned away to make preparations.

Jack heard him go, so he raised his head and tried to roll to one side and get up. Dizziness took control and then darkness overcame him as he passed out again.

CHAPTER 22

<u>*Tuesday, 6:30AM - The Cursed animosity of inanimate*</u>
<u>*Duct Tape*</u>

AMANDA **H**AD BEEN THINKING about her nightmare in duct tape for almost an hour now, and she had finally formulated a plan. Over and over again she'd been moving her feet and ankles up and down, up and down, trying to loosen the duct tape from the legs of the chair. If she could just get the sticky part of the tape to slide up and down, then maybe she'd be able to slide her feet down below the chair legs, thereby freeing herself to at least hobble around the room. It took twenty minutes of nonstop work, but the duct tape finally moved freely up and down on both chair legs. But then she had a new problem. How could she get the duct tape down far enough to slide them totally off the bottom of the chair leg to free her ankles.

She was tempted to give up, totally discouraged, but then she looked into the eyes of the picture on the wall again and kept thinking. That's when she heard a loud crash from somewhere downstairs. Then some thrashing and a few screams and yells. And then ... a gunshot.

And that's when she wondered ... *Is Jack dead now? Is he really gone?* If so, then he really won't be saving me anytime soon.

In desperation, she began rocking her chair back and forth,

trying to get it to tip over, but the chair wouldn't quite tip all the way. Then she tried throwing herself from side to side in an effort to get it to rock. Just before she was about to give up, she felt the two chair legs to her right leave the carpeted floor. They came down quickly again, but she continued throwing herself from side to side, over and over again, each time the chair legs came off the floor just a bit more. She started to tire, but forced herself to continue on. Like a pendulum, she swung back and forth until ... She went over on her right side with a crash. The side of her head hit the floor hard, and she was out cold.

Tuesday, 7:45AM - A Room with a View

"WHAT ARE YOU DOING DOWN THERE, AMANDA?"

Bobbie Lee stood in front of the door, looking down at Amanda's unconscious body, lying motionless on the carpet. He shook his head from side to side as he walked over to her. "That's got to be the dumbest thing I've ever seen, Amanda." Both sides of his face were swollen, leaving his eyes open just a slit. By now Amanda was awake, and she looked up at him, barely able to focus her eyes due to the incredible headache she'd given herself. Two concussions in one week were apparently too much for one person.

"Oh, Hi Bobbie Lee. I was just taking a nap."

He laughed out loud at her remark. "You two sure are turning out to be a real hoot, I'll tell ya!" He continued shaking his head from side to side. "First Jack and now you."

He reached down and grabbed the back of the chair and lifted it back on all four legs effortlessly. "Well, I hope you got enough sleep, because the big show is about to begin. I'm going to kill Jack now, and I'm going to let you watch, out of the goodness in my heart." He tried to smile, but winced in pain,. "I'm even going to give you a ringside seat."

Amanda felt a pang of hope when she heard him say that. *So Jack isn't dead ... at least not yet.* Then, when she saw the condition of Bobbie Lee's face, she couldn't help but goad him. "Looks like you just lost a fight with a giant meat grinder."

He tried to smile again, but couldn't pull it off. "Yeah, but you should see the other guy."

Amanda's head was killing her, and her vision was blurry now for a second before focusing. The pain was excruciating. He grabbed the back of the chair with both sides, tilted her back and drug both her and the chair over to the window. He positioned her in front of the glass and pointed down on the snow-covered lawn.

"Speaking of the other guy. Look down there."

Amanda stared in horror at Jack Ruger, who was tied with ropes to a large diameter railroad tie that had been set up as the vertical post for a clothesline. There was a two-by-four cross beam about five feet off the ground with ropes running out the back side toward another post about thirty feet away.

Jack was naked to the waist, with blood streaming down his face and chest. His feet were bare, and he wore only blue jeans from the waist down. His head hung down onto his chest, and it was impossible to tell if he was dead or alive.

"What have you done to him!"

Amanda shrieked in horror and began to cry, tears running uncontrollably down her face despite the pain beating away inside her head. She stared down for a moment, but then had to turn away, unable to look at him in his present condition.

"This is what happens when people disappoint me, Amanda. Now I want you to watch and learn!"

He reached down with his right hand from behind her and grabbed her jaw to pull it up, forcing her to look at Jack. "There he is ... the mighty Jack Ruger!"

Amanda jerked her head down, latching onto Bobbie Lee's hand with her teeth, She bit down as hard as she could, drawing blood and refusing to let go. Bobbie Lee screamed in pain but couldn't free himself until he punched her in the back of the head with his free hand. Amanda slumped forward again until her chin rested calmly on her chest. Bobbie Lee pulled his hand back, cradling the bleeding hand in his free palm.

He left the room and went into the bathroom. He cleaned up the bleeding fingers and put on several large band aids before the bleeding finally stopped. He filled up the plastic waste basket with cold water and walked hurriedly back into the room. He poured it over Amanda's head until she jerked herself awake, sputtering beneath the steady flow of water. Bobbie Lee lowered the plastic container and threw it on the floor beside her.

"And now you can watch your boyfriend die!"

Tuesday, 8AM, Overwatch

Bobbie Joe Napier watched the spectacle from thirty feet up in his pine tree. He had looked on as Bobbie Lee had tied Jack to the crossbeam of the clothesline post. And he'd wondered _Should I just shoot the bad guy now?_ But he couldn't remember the rules that Jack had explained to him on when he could shoot and when he couldn't, though he suspected right now Jack might forgive him should he err on the side of over-aggression. He didn't want to get in trouble, so he'd held off. Then his view had switched up to the second floor bedroom as the curtains came open. He'd watched as a woman tied to a chair was dragged over in front of the glass. He pulled up his rifle scope and peered through it, centering the crosshairs on Bobbie Lee's head. It was an easy shot but ... was he justified in using deadly force?

Once again, he'd decided to wait. The captain would be here soon, and he could make the decision. Bobbie Joe never had been much of an independent thinker, someone who possessed a high degree of critical thinking skills. At the shop, he just did what he was told and then collected a paycheck. He picked up his radio and tried to get through again, but no one answered him. Should he go down there and cut Jack loose?

He was still thinking about that when he saw the garage

door open up and Bobbie Lee walk out.

Tuesday 8AM, Captain Sterling's Cavalry

JOHNNY STERLING KEPT TRYING TO RAISE BOBBIE JOE on the radio, but to no avail. Something was wrong with his com gear, but he just didn't know what it was. They were still about fifteen minutes out, and he feared they wouldn't make it in time. He reached down and picked up his cell phone. No bars. He should have called the county dispatch when still back in Jackpine, but truth be told, he didn't want the hassle of dealing with law enforcement. They just didn't understand the militia and their unusual methods.

There was a second reason as well. Johnny didn't want them getting in the way. They would treat it like a crime scene, but Johnny knew the truth. This wasn't a crime scene; this was a war zone. And the rules of engagement were simple. Find Jack and the girl and set them free. Then kill Bobbie Lee Harper.

The captain thought about that for moment. Then he re-phrased it in his mind. No, he would kill Bobbie Lee first, and then set Jack and the girl free. This man had been tried and sentenced already at tax payer expense, so why waste more valuable time and money. He'd do it the way they had in the old west. Quick and speedy.

Johnny looked out behind him at the caravan following. It was twenty trucks strong with forty well-armed men and women. He nodded his head and thought to himself *Yep. That oughtta do it.*

"WELL, JACK. I GUESS THIS IS THE PART WHERE YOU AND I say our good byes. Then I shoot you and ride off into the sunset with the pretty girl."

But Jack didn't say anything. His head was lowered onto his chest. Bobbie Lee stepped forward and put his ear to Jack's sternum and listened. Then he reached down into the

165

snow and scooped up a handful of the white powder. He stood up and rubbed the cold snow into Jack's face and eyes.

"Wake up, Jack! Time to be the hero again. Ya gotta save the girl if you can!"

Jack's head raised up slowly. His whole body felt numb from the cold, which was good, because the pain was lessened. He tried to open his eyes again, but they were still caked shut with dried puss and fluid.

"I'm starting to dislike you, Bobbie Lee."

Bobbie Lee laughed out loud as hard as he could. He'd taken some prescription pain killers he'd found inside the house, so he was able to move again without the hassle of pain.

He got up real close to Jack's face and spoke softly into his ear. "I can relate to that, Jack, because I've been hating you for five years now. I've been living and breathing hatred. It's like a molten mixture inside my veins, and not only does my mind hate you, but my heart and my soul, every molecule of my body, every cell, every organ, every nerve, every electron in my body wants to see you die."

Jack lifted his head up slowly and smiled. "So ... you're saying that you don't like me anymore?"

Bobbie Lee smiled right back at him. "You're a funny man right up to the end aren't you?" He reached back and pulled a pistol from the small of his back. He pressed the mag release button, looked at the full magazine and then rammed it back in place. It was Jack's Walther Match Q5 with the blue trigger.

Bobbie Lee pulled on Jack's trouser waistband and shoved the gun inside. "I've never seen a gun like this before with a blue trigger. Weirdest damn thing."

He looked into Jack's swollen face, then slapped him softly on the cheek. Jack didn't even wince.

"Any last words, Jack?" Jack said nothing. "Well, I promised you pistols at dawn, and we both got pistols. Never let it be said that I shot an unarmed man." He looked up at the bedroom window and waved to Amanda. She turned away and Bobbie Lee smiled again.

"That Amanda. She's a real spitfire. I'm going to enjoy her. I promise you that."

Jack tried to open his eyes, but couldn't. "She's watching you right now, Jack. She's going to see you die. You were her saviour, and she's going to watch you die on a cross. That's irony, Jack." Bobbie Lee hacked up some phlegm and spit into Jack's face. "I love it!"

Bobbie Lee pulled the Glock nine millimeter out of the front of his waistband and checked for ammo. "Yep! I got rounds. You got rounds. The sun is up. It's time to close the page on this chapter of our lives and move on." And then he stepped closer and placed the gun against Jack's temple. "The only difference between you and me, Jack, is longevity. I'm going to live, and you're going to die."

He put the Glock pistol back in his waist band and turned to walk away from him.

AMANDA CRIED FROM ATOP HER TOWER, WATCHING Jack hang there on the cross, suspended helplessly, waiting to die. She briefly turned back to the picture of Jesus on the wall, then back out to Jack on the cross. And she wondered ... *What is the difference?*

Tears ran down her cheeks as she prayed one last time. "Please God. Please. Save him. Save Jack."

She watched Bobbie Lee's back as he walked toward the treeline at the edge of the yard. *Where was he going? Was he leaving them? Had her prayers been answered?*

BOBBIE JOE NAPIER LOOKED DOWN AT THE SCENE UN-folding in front of him in amazement. He'd never seen anything like this before ... not even in a movie. Bobbie Lee was walking in his direction now, so he stayed motionless so as not to be discovered. But then the man stopped at the edge of the yard and picked up a rifle that had been leaning against a tree.

Bobbie Joe watched as the man popped out the thirty-round magazine and then quickly slammed it home again. Bobbie Joe quickly raised his own rifle up and found a good rest, then a good cheek weld. His right hand moved down to the grip and his left onto the fore end. He purposely slowed his breathing and his heart rate, readying his mind and body for the shot. He found Bobbie Lee's head in the center of the scope, and moved the crosshairs to exactly the right place. He started his trigger press.

Bobbie Lee brought the rifle up and pushed the butt of the stock into his right shoulder. He looked through the scope for just a second and then changed his mind. The rifle came down and he walked five feet to the right. Once there, he moved to the right side of the oak tree and used it as a stabilizing rest. He quickly found Jack's head and centered the crosshairs. It was an easy shot. All he had to do was press the trigger. And there was the added bonus of absolutely no pressure, because if he missed all he had to do was shoot again and again and again. Until ... Jack Ruger was dead.

Bobbie Joe watched in horror as Bobbie Lee's head suddenly disappeared from his rifle scope. *Where had he gone?* He quickly tore his eyes away from the scope and scanned the yard. He couldn't see Bobbie Lee, just the barrel of his rifle protruding out from behind the oak tree. He raised his rifle up again and looked through the scope. He could see the metal barrel, but it was so small at two hundred yards. He knew in his heart that was the kind of shot made for Hollywood movies but ... no one made that shot in real life.

He was already kicking himself for not taking the easy shot when he'd had it. In just a few seconds, Jack Ruger would be dead, and it would be his fault.

And then ... he got an idea. Perhaps the first original idea of his life.

Jack Ruger lifted his head as high as he could get it. And then he squinted his eyes again. The wet snow that Bobbie Lee had rubbed into his eyes had moistened the dried puss enough so that he could open his eyes ... both of them. He looked down at his pistol tucked into his waist band. He strained against the cross beam and the rope, but nothing moved. Jack looked out at Bobbie Lee and watched him move behind the oak tree. It would just be a few more seconds now before he died.

And then he looked up at the bedroom window to Amanda. He smiled and gently nodded his head. She smiled back and nodded as well. And then he turned back to Bobbie Lee and looked him straight in the eyes. All he saw was the scope.

"I'm ready Lord." And then he sighed painfully. "I miss you, Carrie."

The first shot rang out, followed by another, and another, and another. Bobbie Lee flinched and his own shot went left and struck the cross beam to the right of Jack's head. He stepped back involuntarily away from the oak tree and the next shot hit him in the thigh, breaking his femur and blowing blood and bone out onto the snow. He quickly scrambled back to the cover of the tree, dragging his useless leg behind him.

Once behind cover, Bobbie Lee quickly assessed his leg. The femur was broken, and he was losing blood fast. He wasn't going anywhere. He peeked out from behind the tree just in time to get a face full of shredded bark from a three oh eight round. He ducked quickly back out of the way. He had some quick decisions to make. Who ever it was shooting at him was hidden well and was a very good shot. He assumed that the police were already here or would be shortly. And then it hit him. They're taking me back to prison. Bobbie Lee ground his teeth together in rage. That's when he heard a caravan of trucks coming down the road.

He had to choose. If he took the time to wrap his belt around his leg, he would stop the bleeding and live. If he didn't, well, then he would die and that would be the end of it. But what would happen if he lived? He knew the answer to that question. He would go back to Marquette and face trial for a host of new crimes. He peered out passed the tree, at Jack's body hanging on the cross. His hatred rekindled, burning fiery hot, not letting him think clearly. Jack was there for the taking, like a plum on a low-hanging branch. And then everything came clear to him. He refused to live in a world where Jack Ruger still breathed and pumped blood.

Bobbie Lee struggled to his feet, pulling himself by a branch on the oak tree, bearing the pain in his leg, and fighting against the dizziness that was now forming in his head. And then he thought to himself *Thank god for schedule C drugs.* He braced himself against the tree and took aim. Then out loud he said "Die Jack Ruger. Die and burn in hell!"

Jack felt the bullets ripping into the crossbeam to his right, sending chips of two-by-four to the side of his head. Four shots rang out, and then ceased. He looked over at the crossbeam and saw the chewed-up wood where Bobbie Joe Napier had aimed.

Jack summoned his last bit of resolve and strength and pulled with his right arm until the two-by-four broke in half where the shots had weakened it. The crossbeam came down with a crash as Jack rolled to his left, and quickly took up position of cover behind the railroad tie. Bobbie Lee's bullets started to hit the main post, but couldn't penetrate the thick wood of the railroad tie.

Jack removed the rope attaching his left hand to the crossbeam and then reached down and grabbed the grip of his Q5 and pulled it out, gripping it firmly with both hands. His broken hand cried out in pain, but he fought through it. He could feel the bullets slamming into the wood in front of him and see the muzzle flash from Bobbie Lee's rifle. He worked to focus his eyes on the target. It was a long shot ... a very long shot.

Jack leaned against the post, showing only what parts of him needed showing in order to make the shot. He braced himself, took in a deep breath and let it out slowly. He firmed up his grip, then moved out just a tad. Aim small. Miss small. The red dot on his RMR holographic sight reached out and centered on Bobbie Lee's body. He blinked some blood out of his eyes and started his trigger press.

CHAPTER 23

BOBBIE **L**EE FELT THE FIRST ROUND hit him in the left hand, causing him to drop the rifle to the snow. The next round came two seconds later and hit him square in the chest, but he grabbed onto the tree, refusing to go down. Then another bullet hit his right shoulder, then another in the chest.

He looked down at the snow and all he could see was a blur of white with red blotches. Bobbie Lee coughed, and some red foam came out and dropped onto the snow as well. He looked in Jack's direction, wanting to get one last glimpse of the man who was killing him, but ... his eyesight was already beginning to fail.

He felt himself starting to slide down the tree trunk, feeling the rough bark against his face. He resisted it, but no matter how hard he tried, he couldn't slow his descent. Bobbie Lee's face hit the cold snow, and his cheek rested there. And that's when it hit him.

He'd been killed by a blind man, with a gun that he'd placed in his own hand. And then his last thought this side of death and damnation.

This was ... irony.

AMANDA **W**ALKER LOOKED DOWN FROM ON HIGH AT the carnage below her. Jack was leaning heavily against the railroad tie, and then he began to slip. He caught himself with his left hand, but then caromed off the post and fell to the snow.

Amanda wanted to scream, but she couldn't. Her screams were all gone. Her tears were dried up. She let her head sag one more time to rest upon her chest while the yard below filled with rescuing militia. And then, as an afterthought, she turned her head and looked at the picture on the wall. She could hear people coming up the stairs now.

"Thank you, Jesus. I'll never doubt you again."

CAPTAIN **S**TERLING STOOD OVER **J**ACK **R**UGER WHO WAS being worked on by his medic. "Jack! Can ya hear me, Jack?" But Jack didn't answer. Johnny moved down closer and spoke into his ear. "Jack, the ambulance is on the way, and ya need to hold on. Just five more minutes, Jack."

But Jack didn't hear him. He was deep in a dream. And he saw Carrie there, in her pink bath robe, kneeling over him, her face like an angel. And he said to her. "I love you, sweetheart. I'll always love you." And Carrie smiled softly and kissed him on the forehead. "I love you too, Jack. I'm watching over you, honey. I will always love you,"

Johnny Sterling looked over at his medic, who was taking Jack's vitals and assessing the injuries. "What did he just call me?"

"I think he called you, Sweetheart, sir. He says he'll always love you."

Johnny smiled and then laughed out loud. Then he looked down at Jack, shaking his head from side to side. "I love ya too, Jack. But don't let it go to yer head."

Just then the ambulance pulled in followed by two state cruisers and three sheriff's cars. Captain Sterling knew that some really bad smelling stuff was about to hit the fan, and there would be some explaining that needed to happen. He saw the sheriff and went to him first.

"What the hell is going on here, Johnny!"

Johnny smiled and pointed over at Jack. "Chief Ruger is over there gettin' medical attention. He's gonna need a hospital." Then he pointed over at Amanda who was being carried out of the house on a stretcher. "Amanda Walker is right there. Minor wounds, but she's gonna need the hospital as well."

"Where's Bobbie Lee Harper?"

Johnny pointed over to the treeline where three of his men were staring down at the body. "He's over there. No hurry though. He ain't goin' no place any time soon. Least wise not of his own accord."

The sheriff glanced over at the body. "Who shot him?"

Johnny nodded his head in Jack's direction. "The chief got 'em. Got 'em real good too. Damn he's a good shot."

The sheriff's eyes narrowed. "Were any of your men involved?"

Johnny smiled, raising both palms up in a shrug. "No way man. We just now got here." And then he walked away and gathered up his people for the drive back to Flo's diner and a good, hearty and well-deserved lunch.

The sheriff nodded suspiciously. Then he walked over to check on Jack who was being loaded into the ambulance. He asked the EMT. "Is he gonna make it?"

The man shrugged. "Probably. But we're in a hurry, sheriff. Meet us in Marquette."

AMANDA WATCHED FROM HER STRETCHER AS THEY worked on Jack. She had an IV in her arm, and her head was throbbing with too much pain to bear. When they got to the hospital, she'd have to remember to tell them about her broken collarbone, but right now all she could think of was Jack. She continued to pray silently. Fifteen minutes later Jack began to mumble.

Amanda reached over to him, but it was too far across the aisle. "I'm here, Jack. I'm right beside you. I'm not going anywhere."

He moved his head to his right to look at her. Then he smiled. "I told you I'd save you, Amanda."

She smiled and tears once again began to flow down her cheeks. "I knew you would, Jack. I never doubted you."

Jack closed his eyes a moment, then looked back over at her. "You having a good day yet, Amanda?"

She tried to sit up, but couldn't. It broke her heart to see him like this. His face was so swollen she barely recognized him. And then she put on her very best New York City smile, and said to him as sweetly as she could.

"Every day's a good day in Jackpine."

Jack went to sleep. Amanda just watched over him, enjoying the ride.

CHAPTER 24

Three Days Later - The Dinner

AMANDA LOOKED ACROSS THE TA-
ble at Jack. The puffiness in his face had gone
down now, but the bruises were likely to be there
for several weeks to come. His broken hand was in a cast,
but it was a simple break, and that would heal up as well.
Jack's biggest problem were his broken ribs, and they would
be painful for quite a while until they managed to heal completely. Amanda had tried to get him to take his pain medica-
tion, but he'd refused outright, saying they dulled his senses,
and he wanted to be aware of what was going on around him.
Amanda didn't understand him. She'd taken all her pain meds
and then asked for more.

"So what are you going to do, Amanda?" Jack was sitting
up in his bed, and Amanda was beside him in a chair. She
was wearing a collarbone brace, and didn't like the restrictive
feel of it. The doctors said it was a bad break, that it could
have sheered off and caused even more damage, perhaps even
death, if she hadn't been treated when she was. Her head still
ached, but there was no swelling on her brain, and they said
she would heal up fine.

"I have options."

Jack didn't say anything. There was a food tray in front
of him and another in front of Amanda. Their promised and

long-awaited romantic dinner consisted of fish sticks, green beans, bread and butter and a glass of milk. For desert, they were having Jello. Amanda had blue and Jack the green.

"You really know how to treat a girl, Jack. I don't think I've eaten like this since the fifth grade."

Jack laughed softly. "I had the chefs here whip up something exotic. I told them it was a special occasion."

"I see that. You're becoming quite a celebrity around here. Capturing escaped convicts, rescuing ladies in distress and making impossible shots with your pistol. I feel in awe just being close to you."

Jack sighed. "I know. It's my burden to bear. It's not easy being a lowly public servant. But ..." He looked down for a moment, then back up into her eyes. "I wish it could have been different, Amanda. I wish ..."

She reached over and clasped her hands over his own. "I know, Jack. I understand." And then her next words broke her heart. "You're not ready yet."

A tear welled up in Jack's eye, but he refused to let it fall, willing it back into his body. "I'm sorry. You're a wonderful girl, Amanda. And you deserve a man who can love you without reservation, someone who's not broken, someone who isn't still in love with a ghost."

Amanda cried for just a moment, and then sealed them off for the time being. There would be plenty of time for that later on.

"I called my boss last night and resigned from Bedrock Publishing, effective immediately."

Jack looked surprised. "Are you sure that's what you want to do, Amanda. I thought you loved that job."

She shrugged her shoulders and moved her hands back onto her lap. "I love publishing, but the job at a big city publisher was a bit of a pain at times. Lots of competition, back biting, people trying to hurt you just to get the next promotion. I played that game as well as anyone, but ... I never really enjoyed it. And after a week in Jackpine, I gotta say that I'm a changed woman, Jack."

Jack cocked his head to one side and gave her a quizzical look. "How so?"

She looked down at her green beans and then out the window at all the snow. "You folks have something special here. You watch out for each other." She looked him squarely in the eyes for the next sentence. "You are people of very small pretense."

Jack laughed out loud. "Now there's a word I don't hear much around Jackpine."

"Well, you know it's true, Jack. Take Florence for instance. That woman is blunt, but ... she's also loving about it. She tells you straight up what she's thinking, but she'd also go the extra mile to help a friend. My life has been lacking that, and I'd like to find it somewhere."

Jack's next words were almost a desperate plea. "Have you ever thought about staying on in Jackpine?"

Amanda smiled. "Would you like that? I mean really, Jack? Having a jilted lover hanging around such a small town. It would be clumsy. And you know how these small towns are ... people would talk."

Jack smiled again. He looked out at the snow and the blowing wind outside his room.

"I suppose."

"I need to move on, Jack."

There was a clumsy silence. Jack reached over to take her hand, and they both silently watched the snow in the field across from the hospital.

"Amanda, I gotta tell you. If I was ready ... I'd be all over you like a chicken on a june bug."

Amanda laughed out loud and squeezed his hand."Jack, I don't think a man's ever said that to me before."

Jack waited a few more seconds, enjoying the presence of a beautiful woman who cared for him. He was going to miss that. He hadn't felt this way since ... Carrie. And he briefly wondered if he was doing the right thing.

"So, dear Amanda. What next."

A warm smile brightened her face as she spoke. "I love publishing, Jack, and I have no intention of leaving it. I'm taking a job with a literary agency in New York. They're a small agency, but the people are nice, and they made me a good offer."

She reached down to the floor and pulled up her leather satchel. Amanda took the papers out and handed them to Jack. "I'd like to start by signing you as my first author."

Jack didn't say anything. He didn't know what to say.

"You're a good writer, Jack. You've proven it, and you have so many good stories to offer the public. Let me try and sell your work."

Jack thought about it. It had its pros and cons. "So who is this contract for? Jack Ruger ... or Sara Sinai?"

Amanda motioned with her eyes to the paper. "Just read the contract and think about it. You can be Jack Ruger or Sara Sinai. I don't really care. I accept you the way you are."

But Jack had no intention of reading the contract. "I don't need to read it, Amanda. I trust you."

She handed Jack a pen and he signed.

EPILOGUE

<u>***Two Months Later - Jackpine Diner***</u>

"**M**ORNIN' JACK. THE USUAL?"

Jack walked up to the counter and sat on a bar stool. The cast was off his hand and the bruises on his face had healed completely. His ribs were still tender, but they would be fine with time.

"I'll be drinking it here, Flo. Maybe some bacon and eggs with it too. Whole wheat toast if you don't mind."

Florence looked at him a bit surprised. "Really?"

Jack nodded. "Yep."

Florence pulled out a white, glass mug and poured him a cup of black coffee before handing it to him. She was happy to see him eating better now. Paul Butler, the mayor of Jackpine was sitting off to Jack's right three bar stools down the counter.

"You staying dry, Paul?"

Paul glanced up from his hash browns and ketchup. His pot belly brushed up against the counter. "I never touch the stuff. You know that, Jack."

Jack smiled and blew the steam off his coffee. "That's the spirit, Paul. Keep up the good work."

"Flo, you wanna make those eggs over easy today? I feel like breaking the yolk and dipping my toast in it, just for a change."

Jack and Paul sat quietly at the counter, Jack sipping his coffee, Paul eating his potatoes. Ten minutes later Florence came out with Jack's food and placed it on the counter in front of him. Jack dug right in.

"Do you know what day it is, Jack?"

Jack stopped eating and looked up at her. "Well, it's Saturday, right?"

Florence laughed. "Well, yeah. it's Saturday, but it's Groundhog Day, Jack."

Jack nodded. "Oh, yeah. I guess it kind of snuck up on me this year. You gonna watch that Bill Murray movie again like you do every year?"

Florence nodded. "You betchya. That guy's so funny. And I just love the way he starts out bad and turns into such a good guy at the end. It gives me hope, ya know?"

Jack smiled and took another bite of his bacon. "Yep. I know."

"I'm gonna wheel out the big TV screen 'n show the movie right here like I did last year ya know."

Paul Butler looked over at them. "Ain't no groundhog's up here gonna see their shadow. It's too dern cold."

Jack nodded his agreement. "You got that right, Paul. Those Pennsylvania groundhogs got an easy life I think." Then he looked up at Florence. "So are you going to cook up groundhog to serve tonight? It sure was good last year."

Florence nodded and pointed to the kitchen with a dirty rag. "Yep. I got it in the slow cooker right now. Tom got me a big one back in August. I cut it in half. Gonna cook half fer dinner and tomorrow use the other half fer makin' pasties."

Jack caught himself smiling. He thought of Amanda Walker now in New York city, working as a literary agent. And he couldn't help but ask himself *What would Amanda think about them eating groundhog for dinner tonight?* He laughed out loud and Florence looked at him with a smile on her face.

"What's so funny there, Jack?"

He moved the egg around on his plate. Then he took some toast and sopped up the yoke. "Oh nothing much. Just had a thought."

Florence used her dirty, wet dish rage to wipe up some of the crumbs from around Jack's plate.

"Must a been a doozy!"

And then she added softly. "It's good ta see ya back again, Jack. I been missin' yer smile."

Jack finished his meal and left a ten-dollar bill on the counter. He got up quickly and wiped his mouth on the napkin.

"Gotta go, Flo."

She called out after him. "Ya gonna be back at seven fer the movie?"

Jack was already at the door. The bell rang as he opened it. "I wouldn't miss it for the world, Flo. I'll be here."

Florence waved as he left. "Have a good day, Jack."

Jack smiled. "Every day's a good day in Jackpine, Flo."

And then he was gone.

Florence looked out the window and watched him get into his SUV and drive away. Then she thought out loud as she wiped the counter down.

"I tell ya. If I was twenty years younger 'n better lookin'"

But before she could finish her thought, Paul interrupted her.

"Well, ya ain't so ya can't so just stop yer yappin' about it and get back to work."

Florence looked over at him with a sly smile. "Howd'ya like yer hash browns burnt to a crisp tomorrow?"

He looked back at her and laughed affectionately. "Ya know I can't wait to taste those groundhog pasties, Flo. I think yer pretty near the best cook in Jackpine."

Florence looked out the window at the cold and snow, the wind just as strong today as it was yesterday. Not everyone could live in Jackpine. It took a strong person and a tough breed to handle the long, harsh winters. But then she smiled again. Today was a good day. But then again ...

Everyday was a good day in Jackpine.

Skip Coryell lives with his wife and children in Michigan. He works full time as a professional writer, and *Jackpine Strong* is his thirteenth published book. He is an avid hunter and sportsman, a Marine Corps veteran, and a graduate of Cornerstone University. You can listen to Skip as he co-hosts the syndicated military talk radio show *Frontlines of Freedom* on frontlinesoffreedom.com. You can also hear his weekly podcast *The Home Defense Show* at homedefenseshow.com

For more details on Skip Coryell, or to contact him personally, go to his website at skipcoryell.com

Stay Tuned for book 2 in the
Jack Ruger adventure series.

Books by Skip Coryell

We Hold These Truths
Bond of Unseen Blood
Church and State
Blood in the Streets
Laughter and Tears
RKBA: Defending the Right to Keep and Bear Arms
Stalking Natalie
The God Virus
The Shadow Militia
The Saracen Tide
The Blind Man's Rage
Civilian Combat - The Concealed Carry Book
Jackpine Strong

Made in the
USA
Lexington, KY